Payback Canyon

Due to a combination of laziness and bad judgement, sheep farmer Wiley Hansen is broke. He tells his daughter Grace that he has arranged paid work for her on a neighbouring farm. She willingly agrees in order to help the family finances, but in reality he intends to put her up for auction in the local saloon. Grace manages to escape, however, when the auction is disrupted by the arrival of a notorious outlaw.

Believing Grace has been kidnapped, her brother Joe sets out to find her and bring her home. When Joe does eventually discover where his sister is, what he finds is far from what he expects.

Payback Canyon

Rob Hill

A Black Horse Western

ROBERT HALE

© Rob Hill 2020
First published in Great Britain 2020

ISBN 978-0-7198-3083-9

The Crowood Press
The Stable Block
Crowood Lane
Ramsbury
Marlborough
Wiltshire SN8 2HR

www.bhwesterns.com

Robert Hale is an imprint
of The Crowood Press

The right of Rob Hill to be identified as
author of this work has been asserted by him
in accordance with the Copyright, Designs and
Patents Act 1988

Typeset by
Derek Doyle & Associates, Shaw Heath
Printed and bound in Great Britain by
4Bind Ltd, Stevenage, SG1 2XT

For Val

1

Wiley Hansen barged open the saloon door and shoved his daughter inside. The sound of conversation died: everyone was expecting them. The girl, Grace, was tall like her father, with his pinched face and pale eyes. The lines in her face made her look older than her eighteen years. Her dark hair was tied back under a gingham bonnet, she wore a faded cotton house dress, and her hands were red raw from chores. She looked as though she could do with a good meal. She stiffened when she felt the men's eyes on her, glanced towards her father for reassurance. Hansen tightened his grip on his daughter's arm and marched her forwards.

Like his daughter, Hansen was thin and possessed the kind of wiry, muscular strength that hard living gives. The frayed edges of his jacket had been carefully repaired, his woollen work shirt had been darned many times, and his boots were nearly worn through. Clearly nervous, he signalled the bartender for a whiskey. There was a handgun, an old Colt Patterson five-shot, shoved awkwardly behind his belt buckle. It looked as if it was there for show.

'Money first, Wiley,' the barman said. He didn't trouble himself to put down the glass he was cleaning.

Fifteen men or thereabouts, had they come just to gawp or to buy? Hansen wondered. He knew all of them. Sodbusters, sheep farmers, the one or two who owned a few head of beef cattle, and the men who worked the river crossing. Most of them had started out on the Oregon Trail a few years ago, got this far and lost heart: some had planned their journey so poorly that they ran out of supplies; some had overloaded their wagons, which meant they fell apart; some had been robbed and left with nothing. Unable to tolerate the gruelling conditions, one or two of their wives had run off to join men on more prosperous trains; some of their children had died. Since they ended up here at Backwater, the town that had sprung up on this bend in Gunn River, none of them had done more than eke out a living.

There was one exception. At the table nearest

the bar, Jehu Cloake sprawled back in his chair with his legs stretched out in front of him. A tough, ruddy-faced sheep farmer, he was heavily built and strong. He wore a well-cut black jacket and expensive boots, the chain of a fob watch looped between the pockets of the vest that stretched over his round stomach. The top of the brass pocket telescope he used for keeping an eye on his flock peeped out of his jacket pocket. Chewing slowly on a plug of tobacco, he watched Hansen and the girl with a contemptuous stare. He was used to getting what he wanted.

'Gun, Wiley,' the barman prompted.

Beside the door was a row of wooden pegs where the customers hung their gun belts, new Navy Colts and old Patterson five-shots.

Hansen ignored him.

A murmur of conversation picked up. It was obvious the men were all talking about Grace. There was puzzlement in the air, disapproval, as though she shouldn't be here. They stared Wiley down for bringing her.

'Pa,' Grace turned to him. The atmosphere made her uneasy. She had thought about what her father had proposed and agreed to it because she believed it would be better for all three of them – her pa, her brother Joe and herself. In the years since her mother had passed away, the farm had run back. Since the disaster last winter when their entire flock had frozen to death up on the high pasture, they had nothing. She did her best to keep house, and hadn't got it in her to blame her pa for spending his days at his still at the back of the barn or his nights drinking. If it wasn't for Joe's skill with the hunting rifle and her ability to make do and mend, the three of them would have starved.

You could go and work for another family, one of the neighbours, Hansen had told his daughter. It wouldn't be so bad. I'd arrange it. Just for a few weeks, a month or two at most, everyone's busy at this time of year. You'd get proper wages, I'd make sure of that; you'd get bed and board, so that would be an extra saving. Joe could concentrate on his traps and sell the pelts. I'd work on fixing up the farm.

At first, Grace was unsure – her father had had money-making schemes in the past that came to nothing. But she knew that they were in dire straits and saw the sense in his plan. She could put up with anything if it was just for a few weeks, couldn't she? Dutiful girl that she was, she agreed. Just don't tell your brother, Hansen added. Knowing how fond Joe was of her, and that he was bound to oppose any plan which meant she had to leave home, Grace agreed to that, too.

That had been a few days ago. But now, standing here in the saloon with her father gripping her arm, things didn't feel right. Her pa had assured her that they would meet whoever was going to take her on, at the saloon. He didn't want to tell her who it was, he said, as there might be some discussion over her wages, nothing was finalized yet. Grace accepted this, as she always accepted what her pa said. Anyway, she had known all the neighbours since childhood. None of them lived more than a few miles from her home. What was there to worry about?

'We all know why we're here.' Wiley cut through the conversation.

'I'll bid a dollar,' someone shouted from the back.

There was an embarrassed silence. Grace looked at her father. Bid? Had she heard right? His grip on her arm was starting to hurt.

Wiley laughed uneasily. 'Come on, now.'

'I'll take her.' The gravel voice belonged to Jehu Cloake.

Grace didn't like him. His stern, unsmiling face and his cruel stare unnerved her. His wife Sarah had always been kind, but she had run off and left him the previous summer and now Cloake lived alone.

Cloake was well known as a hard-working sheep

11

farmer. But Grace had heard the rumours about the other way he made his money. Each spring he rode out to meet the wagon trains as they passed his farm and convinced the emigrants that their skinny longhorns would be worthless in California. There were already beeves a-plenty there, fat and healthy after being reared on lush grass, he said, and dog cheap. Anyway, their animals would be unlikely to survive the climb up to the high plains and through the mountain passes beyond. They were more trouble than they were worth. He would be doing the owners a favour by taking them off their hands. Cloake never paid more than a knock-down price, and the more gullible even handed over their precious livestock for nothing.

Everyone knew Cloake was the richest man in the room, so bidding against him would be a waste of time. Besides that, no one ever wanted to cross him. 'Ten bucks.' He waved his hand dismissively towards Grace. Two of the fingers were missing.

Grace stared at each of the men's faces. What was going on? This wasn't what her father had said.

She pulled at his arm. 'Pa?'

'Shut up, Gracie.' Hansen called across to Cloake: 'Come on, Jehu. You can do better than that.' But he didn't sound convinced.

'Pa, what's going on?'

'Gracie, I've told you.' Hansen tightened his

grip on his daughter's arm. There was an edge to his voice, irritation with Grace for not keeping quiet, fear that Cloake was going to get one over on him and his plan would fail.

'Don't hear any other bids. Do you, Wiley?' Cloake made a pretence of looking innocently round the room.

He was right. There were no other bids. Everyone knew it was wiser not to go up against Cloake, he would outbid them anyway. Instead, the men sat back to enjoy watching Wiley Hansen squirm and to see how his daughter would react. Most of them had known Grace since she was a kid, they understood that it was mainly through her efforts that the Hansen household had stayed afloat since her mother passed. She didn't deserve this. They all knew about Wiley's drinking. He was asking to be ridden over roughshod by Cloake.

'Pa, please.' Grace sounded scared now. Her father had arranged something with these men, but she still couldn't grasp what it was.

'Come on, Jehu.' Hansen tried again.

'Ain't even got enough to afford a shot of red eye, have you Wiley?' Cloake took delight in goading him.

'Fifty,' Hansen said. He knew he was clutching at straws. 'That's fair.'

Cloake laughed again. He was enjoying this. His

13

farm shared a boundary with the Hansen place. It occurred to him that he might be able to get some land as well as the girl if he played his cards right. Hansen was desperate, anyone could see that. On top of that he was a drunk, and on top of that he was a fool. Nothing would give Cloake more pleasure than to grind Hansen's selfish scheme under his boot heel.

Just then, something caught Grace's attention. Up until now, she had been mesmerized by the crowd of men's faces staring at her – the looks they gave her made her skin creep. Men she had known all her life had suddenly become strangers. She had visited all their farms at one time or another, talked to their wives, made friends with their children and run errands for their families whenever they needed her to. Now, for some reason she didn't understand, they were ranged against her. Chalked on the wall was a message:

This Friday noon, auction you all heard about. My daughter, Grace. Highest bidder. Signed W. Hansen.

Grace's blood ran cold.

'Pa. I don't like this. This ain't what we talked about.' She tried to pull away, but Hansen's grip on his daughter's arm was like a vice. He didn't

14

look at her.

'Pa, please.'

'Hush, Gracie. We've all got to do what we can, we've been over it. I'll buy you back in a couple of months, you'll see.'

'What do you mean, buy me back?' Shock knocked the wind out of her.

She wrenched her arm hard but Hansen held on. He had expected this. He faced the men with a grin fixed to his mouth. There was nothing wrong, nothing for anyone to be concerned about, just a filly playing up a little.

'Ten dollars is the price of a breeding ewe.' Cloake watched Grace try to twist her way out of Hansen's grip. 'That's enough to get your farm started again, Wiley.' He spoke deliberately loudly to make sure everyone heard. 'Provided you don't leave her up on the plains and let her freeze to death.'

The men laughed. The slapdash way Hansen ran his farm was well known.

'Pa, are you selling me?' Grace's face was red as the full force of the humiliation hit home. Tears stood in her eyes, the corners of her mouth were turned defiantly down. Anger boiled up inside her.

'Let go of me.' She tried to kick at her father but he held her at arm's length. The men in the saloon laughed aloud. One or two of them cheered her on.

'Ten.' Cloake boomed. 'My final offer.'

'How could you, Pa?' Grace's kicks were landing on Hansen's shins. She hacked at his knees.

'Ten for the girl,' Cloake produced a roll of bills out of his vest pocket, peeled off a ten and slapped it down on the table in front of him. 'Looks to me like she could be more trouble than she's worth.'

Uproar. The men hadn't had fun like this since they couldn't remember when. Some cheered Grace on; others shouted for Hansen to take the money while he had the chance; still more of them yelled for him to demand more. Hansen tried to stare Cloake down. Cloake watched him with a smirk on his face, his hand with the missing fingers held the ten flat on the table. Grace writhed and lashed out; it was all Hansen could do to hold on to her.

The saloon doors burst open. A cowboy stood there, trail dust on his hat and clothes, a Navy Colt at his hip. He was a young guy, square-shouldered and strong. Silence fell like a guillotine. He wore the same work clothes as the other men, but there was an authority about him that none of the others possessed.

'This the auction I've been told about?'

The crowd of men started to part in front of him. Suddenly, everyone wanted their back to be against a wall. The stranger stood face to face with

16

Hansen and Grace. Grace had one last hack at her father's shins and then stood still. Cloake heaved his bulk round to stare.

'You making a bid?' A sly smile flickered at the corners of Hansen's mouth.

'Nope.' The stranger held Hansen's gaze.

'Then she's mine.' Cloake levered himself out of his chair, picked up the ten and tucked it into Hansen's top pocket. 'Bought and paid for.'

'Let the girl go.' The stranger's words were as hard and plain as steel. His hand was ready over the Navy Colt in his belt. When Cloake turned and saw the gun, colour drained from his face, his eyes darted towards his own gun hanging by the door.

With his free hand, Hansen made a grab for the Patterson in his belt. The crowd shrank back, they saw what was going to happen. Cloake launched himself out of the line of fire, crashed against one of the tables and fell. In the time it took for Hansen to bring the five-shot level, the cowboy drew and fired. Hansen tumbled forwards, sending his gun clattering across the wooden floor, releasing his grip on his daughter as he fell. Grace didn't hesitate. She strode over her pa's body, leaped across Cloake, elbowed past the stranger and charged out through the saloon door.

The stranger, gun in hand, stepped forward and slid the ten out of Hansen's pocket. Then he turned to Cloake and pulled the roll of bills out of his good hand. Cloake whimpered as the stranger's Navy Colt brushed the tip of his chin. Then the stranger holstered his sidearm and strode through the door after Grace.

2

'Anyone home?' Cloake's bellow sounded like an angry bull. It was a two-hour ride from town and the afternoon light had already started to fail. He heaved himself down from his horse, flicked the reins across the hitching rail and stomped up the porch steps. 'Joe Hansen, you here?'

Cloake pressed his face to the window and peered in. Not much to see inside – a stove, wooden table, hard chairs. The room was swept and tidy. A neatly folded pile of blankets showed where someone slept on the floor by the stove. Cooking pots polished to a shine were stacked on the floor. A sheet was hung up to divide off a corner of the room: Grace must sleep in there, while Wiley and his son slept behind.

'Hey. Anyone here?' Cloake moved the plug of tobacco in his mouth. 'Joe Hansen, you got that sister of yours here?'

He shoved open the door and cast his eye round the room. The air was cold inside. Splits in the cottonwood walls needed repair. There was ash in the stove. A hunting rifle was missing from its pegs over the fire place.

Cloake pushed the cotton sheet aside. There was one narrow bed with a pile of blankets slung across it and another untidy heap on the floor. Apart from that, the room was empty. Cloake scowled. Ten dollars. Plus, he was being made to look a fool. Then he heard something, some slight movement. He slid his Colt out of its holster. The sound came from under the bed. Cloake smiled to himself, he had her now. He dropped awkwardly to his knees and peered under.

Nothing. Just a collection of empty red-eye bottles and a mouse skittering in the dust. Damnit, he felt like blowing the little critter's head off.

Then there was a noise behind him. A footstep. 'What are you doing down there? Who is that?' A young man's voice, accusing at first, then simply puzzled.

'Jehu? Is that you?'

Cloake held out a hand and gestured angrily for Joe to help him to his feet. Joe Hansen stood there staring at the fat old man who seemed to have lost something under his pa's bed. If it wasn't for

Cloake's furious expression and the gun in his hand, Joe would have laughed aloud.

Joe was skinny like his sister and wiry like his pa. His jacket and work shirt were hand-me-downs that had been repaired a good many times. His open face and cheerful smile suggested he was used to his family being poor. It had never occurred to him to do much about it. As long as he had a meal in his belly and somewhere dry to sleep, he was content with the way things were. He held out a hand and hauled Cloake to his feet.

'That sister of yours, is she here?' Cloake was furious.

'Gracie?' Joe stared at him, wide eyed. Jehu Cloake never came out here, and to discover him kneeling on the bedroom floor peering under the bed was too bizarre for words. 'She went into town with Pa.'

'Where the hell is she now?' Cloake stamped back into the other room, his boots banged on the wooden boards. He cast his eye round the cabin, the poverty of the place depressed him. Through the open doorway he could see broken fences and a gate that needed rehanging. Even the chicken coop in the yard stood empty. He was contemptuous of Wiley for letting his place run back like this.

'Where is she?' Cloake brushed the dust off the sleeves of his jacket in an effort to reclaim his dignity after being caught on all fours. 'You got a barn out back?' He headed out of the door and across the yard with Joe trailing in his wake.

'What do you want Gracie for?' Joe couldn't work it out.

'You hiding her?' At the door to the barn, Cloake wheeled round and jabbed a finger. Joe's eyes fell on the empty knuckles and their ugly scars.

'She in here?' Cloake's good hand was on the handle of his colt again. Everyone knew a version of the story of how Jehu Cloake lost his fingers: his wife, Sarah, had taken a shot at him before she ran off. Some people said an argument had spiralled out of control one night, and the handgun she grabbed went off unintended. Others said she sat by the kitchen door for hours cradling a scatter-gun, waiting for Cloake to come home. Some said she aimed to kill him and missed, others that she meant to fire a warning shot and took his fingers by accident. What everyone agreed on was that kindly, tolerant Sarah had had enough of her husband's bullying ways.

Jehu Cloake's temper was legendary – everyone had witnessed his rages at one time or another. He had treated Sarah like a skivvy for years: their cabin was her prison. He became irritated when she left the farm to go to the store, resented her making friends with the wives of the other farmers, expected her to work the farm alongside him and keep the house pristine.

No one was surprised when Sarah lit out. A wagon train bound for California had passed through the previous day, so everyone, Cloake included, assumed that she had caught up with it. He didn't go after her.

'I let her go,' Cloake railed in the saloon that evening, a bottle of red eye in front of him on the bar. The men stared at the bloody bandage wrapped round his hand. 'Better off without her. Worked sunup till sundown every day since I arrived in this godforsaken wilderness, built the best farm around here. Done it all singlehanded, and this is how she thanks me.'

The guys in the saloon had to admit that Jehu Cloake's appetite for hard work was just as legendary as his temper. It was true that his was the most productive farm in the area, his flock of Rambouillets, the tough breed of sheep that thrived despite blazing summers and freezing winters, was the biggest for miles. His boast was that he never lost a single animal. He kept an eagle eye on his flock through the telescope he always carried with him, and had been known to track a stray for days. Added to that, the bargains he drove when it came to buying and selling were the hardest. But he was a bully. No one felt sorry for him for having his fingers shot off. Behind their hands, the men in the saloon that night all agreed that he had it coming.

Cloake barged the barn door open. The hinges had dropped and the weight of the door scraped a groove in the dirt. This was Joe's domain, and the place was a mess. The remains of a hay pile spilled across the floor, there were mouse droppings everywhere, and dark patches stained the earth floor underneath where the roof leaked. A half-scraped deerskin was stretched on a frame in one corner, an old saddle, the leather cracked and dry, sat neglected on the edge of the stall. On the work-bench, beside a can of oil and a pile of rags, a Sharps rifle lay waiting to be cleaned. In one of the stalls, Magic, Joe's Quarter Horse, stood patiently. She was well fed, her glossy coat brushed and shining.

Cloake grunted. 'Where else is there?'

'Look, she ain't here. She went into town with Pa.' Joe could see Cloake was still furious.

'Where does your pa make his red eye?' Cloake turned, pushed past Joe and headed for Wiley's still.

'Come on, Jehu.' Joe started to laugh.

'Shut up, boy.' Cloake rounded on him. 'I bought her. I'm taking her home with me.'

'What are you talking about?' This was non-sense; Joe didn't get it.

The still was under a canvas awning at the back of the barn. Empty bottles were strewn on the ground. There was the sharp smell of the mash in the air. There was a threadbare old chair with horsehair stuffing bursting through the leather, and an old bench you could use as a footstool. No one could see you from the house or the yard here. The chair faced miles of open plain bordered in the distance by soaring mountains. It was a place you could sit and dream.

'What are you talking about, Jehu?' Joe was worried now.

'The auction.' Cloake spat on the ground, taking care to avoid his boots. 'Bought your sister this afternoon, and she damn well ran off.'

'Bought Gracie? What are you talking about?' Joe's stomach turned, he felt sick.

'Don't you worry,' Cloake said. 'I'll find her.' He stared at Joe – the boy's face was white. 'Telling me you didn't know about this?'

Even before Cloake explained, Joe knew this was one of his pa's hairbrained schemes, something he had cooked up with his saloon buddies egging him on, or sitting here in his chair with the red eye making his dreams seem real. Somehow he had managed to persuade Gracie, dear, sweet Gracie, to take part.

'Ten bucks,' Cloake snapped. 'She should be back at my place now. I've been living off trail food since Sarah took off.'

'You paid my pa ten bucks for Gracie?' Joe was incredulous. He believed it and didn't believe it. 'My pa sold her to you?'

'Didn't he tell you?' Cloake's laugh sounded like a bark. He studied Joe for a moment. The boy was weak like his father. He didn't know anything. He probably spent his evenings sitting here by the still with his pa while the fences went unrepaired and there were gaps in the roof. Still, Cloake supposed, they hadn't got a flock to worry about now. He grinned inwardly, thinking of his own sheep, which he would soon lead up to their summer pasture.

'Why don't you fix this place up?' Cloake sneered. 'You got nothing to do now you lost your flock. Just look at it.' He gestured towards the house.

'I'm getting to it,' Joe said. It was embarrassing to have to explain himself, he knew Cloake intended to make him feel small. The truth was that the place had been run down for so long, he hardly noticed any more. His pa never bothered, only Grace complained about the state of the homestead. He was used to his pa ignoring her, so

Joe never paid much attention to her complaints either. It never occurred to him that this might hurt her.

'Spend my time trapping now, putting food on the table that way.' Joe attempted to justify himself. 'Anyway, Pa's working on the house.'

'Not any more he ain't.' Cloake gave another short laugh. He remembered the boundary his farm shared with this place. He wondered how much he could get it for. Better not offer anything right away. He'd find the girl first, give Joe a week or two to realize there was no future for him here, then he should be able to get him to sign it over for next to nothing.

'Your pa's dead, Joe.' He told the story of what had happened in the saloon that afternoon.

Joe's face hardened. He didn't flinch, didn't look away from Cloake. He listened carefully to every word. He saw it all. His pa's underhand scheme, his silver tongue encouraging Grace to take part, persuading her that it would be for her own good, for the good of them all. He could imagine her agreeing right away, bravely facing up to what she believed needed to be done. The two of them had kept it secret from him because they knew he would put his foot down. He would have guarded Grace with his life.

'This guy who shot him. . . .' Joe's voice was

hoarse.

'Rowan Gold,' Cloake said. 'He's a wanted man. They say he raised hell all over Missouri, robbed, murdered, maimed, Lord knows what. Now he's holed up out here in the territories where there's no law to come after him. Some sort of hideout up beyond the high plains, I heard. Only the Shoshone and the mountain men go up there.'

'You saw him take Gracie?' Joe's voice sounded calm, casual almost, no hint of emotion.

'Saw him take my money,' Cloake snarled. 'Your sister just ran outside. When I got there, she was gone.'

He turned away from Joe and started to walk round the back of the house, on the lookout for anywhere Grace might be hiding. There was a garden back there, a square of tended grass, spring flowers just starting to push through. In the centre of the plot was a grave marked with a wooden cross.

'Gracie came out here every day,' Joe said.

Cloake scowled. The girl wasn't here. He'd come on a fool's errand.

'I thought she would have headed home.' Cloake spat on the ground. 'Looks like Gold took her with him.'

3

Before sunup next morning, Joe started down the trail to town. Dreams, thoughts, his head had held a whirlwind all night, he'd not slept at all. Where was Gracie? Why had Gold taken her? How could he get her back? Every time he lay down and pulled a blanket over him, Gracie's sweet face shimmered in front of his eyes, smiling her beautiful smile. A minute later he was awake, bolt upright, soaked in sweat.

Then there was his pa, shot in the saloon, trying to pull off one more lazy scam. What the hell did he think he was doing? And why had Gracie gone along with it? Even though Joe could figure out the answers, the questions burned in his brain like coals.

Unable to sleep, Joe went out to the barn and finished cleaning the Sharps by the light of a tallow candle, wiped down the oiled wood stock and its brass fittings, and set to work on the percussion mechanism and the barrel. He collected up all the ammunition he had and searched out all the shells he could find for his pa's five shot. His first duty was to bury his pa, then he had to find Grace. Someone in the saloon must have a notion where Gold was holed up. He saddled up before dawn.

Backwater was a haphazard collection of cotton-wood buildings clustered around one of the river crossings on the Oregon Trail deep in the territory between South Pass and Fort Bridger. Emigrants on their way to California stopped here to rest their oxen and take advantage of the strip of marshy pasture before tackling the Gunn River. The crossing was difficult enough in the summer months and required the assistance of men from the town with their ropes and knowledge of the shifting riverbed. When the spring thaw was on up on the high ground, it was a torrent.

The Red Eye Saloon was where disputes were argued over and settled. The General Store sold necessities and operated as a market for traders from the east and trappers from the high plains – dry goods and ammunition in exchange for beaver pelts. Not that there was any love lost between the townsfolk and the mountain men. The trappers were a breed apart, a hangover from a bygone age before there were settlers in the territories, before the Oregon Trail had even been thought of. The townsfolk regarded the trappers as uncouth and untrustworthy; the trappers considered the people of Backwater weak-minded money grubbers.

Groups of Shoshone Indians brought buffalo meat into town to trade. They were quiet, dignified men and women who kept themselves to themselves, tolerated being regarded with suspicion, and never outstayed their welcome. In the spring, wagon trains rolled in. The faces of the emigrants shone with relief when they reached even this small outpost. The women headed for the store, the men hung about outside the saloon, and delighted with a respite from the journey, the children played hide and seek under the wagons.

Wiley Hansen's corpse was laid out on a trestle at the back of the saloon. Someone had placed coins respectfully on his eyes. His handgun lay beside him. Joe carried the body through the barroom and tied it across the saddle of his horse outside. He was surprised at how heavy it felt, the dead weight was almost too much for him to lift. But he felt no grief, just deep weariness: his pa had let the farm run back, he had lost their flock, spent their money. Now Grace was gone because he had driven her away.

'I'd like to help you, Joe.' Clive Mulkey was the

owner of the saloon, a tall, narrow-shouldered man with a mournful face. He knew how to handle difficult customers, when to speak and when to be quiet. He believed that the key success in his business was to be a friend to everyone.

Joe pointed to the announcement chalked on the wall.

'Auction you all heard about. My daughter, Grace. What kind of place are you running here?'

'It was something your pa wrote up there. I didn't know nothing about it.' Mulkey shrugged innocently. 'Never told me what he had in mind.'

'Hell you didn't.' A squarely built man sat at a corner table close enough to hear. Dressed in an animal-hide shirt and an old Stetson, a thick black beard covered the lower half of his face. Bowie in hand, he was half way through a plateful of charred buffalo meat. This was Thomas Rust, a trapper from the high plains. One winter, years ago, he and his partner were cut off for four months by the snows high in the Windstorm Mountains. His partner never came down in the spring. The rumour was that Rust survived by eating him.

'Whole town knew.' Rust chewed the meat reflectively. 'Dime to a dollar it was you who told Jehu about it, Mulkey.'

'Everyone knew?' Joe said. 'Everyone?'

'Did Wiley tell you to tell Jehu?' Rust glanced at Mulkey and stabbed another piece of meat. He didn't like towns or the people who lived in them. Clive Mulkey was a particularly spineless example. 'After all, if you're going to sell something, you want somebody in the room who's got money to buy it.'

Mulkey busied himself with a shelf of glasses and seemed not to be listening.

'Where does this Rowan Gold hide out?' Joe came straight out with it. 'That's where she's gone, ain't it?'

'You're going after Gold?' Rust looked at Joe with new interest, maybe he had misjudged him.

Mulkey shifted the glasses on the shelf.

'Got to get my sister back,' Joe said simply.

'Got a hideout up beyond the high plains. No one's ever been there.' Rust speared his last piece of meat. 'If you go near it, he'll know you're coming and shoot you, sure as day.'

Suddenly Joe felt as if his clothes were made of lead. The task was impossible. He looked at the writing chalked on the wall. His pa had planned this. Even though he never spoke ill of the dead, Joe would never forgive him.

'Did Gracie say anything?'

'Not that I heard.' Mulkey carried on wiping glasses. 'Came in with your pa and just stood there.'

'Don't you ever give a straight answer?' Rust glared contemptuously at Mulkey. He wiped his bowie on his sleeve and slid it back in its sheath. 'The girl fought like a wildcat. Your pa held on to her, wouldn't let her go. Looked to me like the whole thing was a surprise to her, like he'd told her one thing to get her here, and when she walked through that door it was something else.'

'Didn't see any of that.' Mulkey shrugged again. 'Not from back here.'

Joe could imagine. From out in the barn, many times he heard his pa bark orders at Grace. Complaints, too much salt in the stew or too little, his words slurred. There was no reasoning with him once the red eye had got hold. One time he blamed her for there not being any chickens in the coop when he had made her kill the last one the previous day. Joe stayed out in the barn and let them get on with it.

Even now, Joe could hear Gracie's patient voice, trying to keep her pa calm. It's only the whiskey talking, she would say later, he never means it. Sure enough, the next day in he would come with a bunch of wild flowers he had collected for her, canary violets, firecracker penstemon, Indian paintbrush, as bright as a handful of fire. Joe would overhear his pa's flannel-mouthed apologies, and Gracie assuring him that everything was

34

all right.

The barn was Joe's workshop and sanctuary. He even slept out there on the straw pile sometimes. Between almost daily hunting trips out on the plains and whole days spent fishing for bullheads and cut-throat trout down at the river he was hardly home at all. Told himself he was feeding the family, making up for his pa's neglect. And of course, he was. Well aware that fences needed mending and repairs needed doing on the house, he also knew he was avoiding confrontation, and letting his sister cope with their pa's wild moods. On the days when his traps were empty, the fish didn't bite and he came home empty-handed, he headed straight for the barn and didn't go into the house at all.

'You didn't have no idea what your pa was up to?' Rust was puzzled.

'Just tell me how to get to Gold's place.' Joe knew what he had to do. Mulkey had been listening all along, now he made no secret of it. He put down the glass he was holding and leaned on the bar.

Before Rust could answer, the saloon door swung back and Jehu Cloake burst in. He was in a foul mood. His mouth was down at the corners, his eyes were like bullets. He went to unbuckle his gun belt and then thought better of it.

'Thought I'd find you here.' He glared at Joe.

Joe didn't answer. Mulkey poured a shot for Cloake without being asked.

'Thought you'd got away with something, didn't you, Jehu?' Thomas Rust leaned back in his chair and eyeballed Cloake. 'Didn't reckon on Gold showing up, did you?'

'That sister of yours come home last night?' Cloake kept his stare fixed on Joe.

'Yeah, she would have come back 'specially just so she could head over to your place.' Rust was enjoying this.

'I'm going to get her back,' Joe said quietly. 'Just as soon as I've buried my pa. She'll be coming home with me. You got no call on her, Jehu.'

Cloake fired down his shot of red eye and slammed his glass on the bar. Mulkey refilled it.

'There's a bar-room full of witnesses saw what happened. I paid my money fair and square.'

'Gold took your money and the girl ran off,' Rust chimed in. 'That's what I saw.'

'Nobody can catch Gold,' Mulkey said. 'He outran the troopers from Fort Caspar on his way out here. If the troopers can't catch him, no one can.'

'Where did you hear that?' Rust put his feet on a chair. This was interesting. He wasn't sure whether he believed it.

'Guy off one of the trains last summer, sat right where you are now. Gold was wanted for killing a guy in Missouri. Word was sent to Caspar to head him off.'

'Figures,' Cloake said. 'I heard he shot a guy over a poker hand. No warning, fella didn't stand a chance.'

Rust was thinking about something.

'If that sister of yours does show up. . . .' Cloake began.

'How come Gold knew about the auction?' Rust interrupted.

Mulkey picked up a glass from behind the bar and began polishing. 'Must have seen the sign.' He nodded to the announcement chalked on the wall.

'He was in here?' Cloake wheeled round.

'A week back,' Mulkey said.

'What was he doing in here?' Rust lifted his feet off the chair and leaned forward.

'Bought some bottles of red eye.' Mulkey put down the glass, picked up another and started polishing.

They waited for him to go on.

'I came in one morning and there he was, asleep with his head on the table. Looked like he'd been riding all night.'

'So?' Cloake prompted.

'Wanted to know all about the farms round

here, who lived where, who owned the sheep up on the high ground.' Mulkey looked nervous, he had to be careful with Cloake.

'My sheep?' Cloake was wrongfooted.

'Not just yours, everyone's,' Mulkey said. 'Paid for his breakfast, then he left.'

'Why was he asking about my sheep? What else did he say?'

'Nothing. Wanted to know who had the best breeders. Maybe he's thinking of keeping some himself.'

'Did he ask about the auction?' Joe nodded towards the words chalked on the wall.

'Saw for himself what was written up there. I told him what the rumours were. Why shouldn't I?' Mulkey could be blunt with Joe.

'He took that roll of bills right out of your hand, Jehu.' Rust couldn't resist one last jibe. 'You intending to raise a posse and go after him?'

'With Gold's reputation?' Cloake looked furious. 'When folks hear he's been in town asking questions, they're going to lock their doors.' He signalled Mulkey for another whiskey, two fingers missing from his hand.

Joe had to get his pa home and buried. Outside, Rust caught up with him.

'You really going after Rowan Gold?'

Joe nodded. His pa's Colt Patterson five shot felt

38

heavy in his belt.

'I'll show you the way,' Rust said. 'I'm headed up to the plains anyway. And you'll need a hand putting your pa in the ground.'

4

Joe and Thomas Rust set out at first light. The cold
air smelled sweet and fresh. Joe tied the Sharps, a
bedroll and all the dried food and coffee he had,
behind his saddle. Rust climbed on his old mule.
The high plains loomed in the far distance, and
beyond them the snowy peaks of the Windstorms.
Jack rabbits dodged in and out of patches of
prairie grass. They surprised a family of elk, which
bounded away through the grey half-light. After
they left the farm, Joe didn't look back.

From the outset, Joe had to rein in Magic to let
Rust's mule keep pace. She was loaded with
months' worth of supplies and ammunition for his
Springfield. Bear traps hung either side of the
saddle, and with Rust's weight as well, progress was
slow. He kept a loose hold on her horsehair reins.

'Tulip comes into her own in the mountains

40

where you're headed,' Rust looked at Magic with an approving eye. 'We could make an exchange later. I'd be doing you a favour.'

Joe's thoughts wandered back over the previous day. Rust announced that he had sold his pelts, stocked up with supplies and ammunition for his trusted Springfield and for the Colt he kept in his boot, and was headed back up to the high plains. Asking no more than a pot of fresh coffee, he had offered to help Joe dig the grave. Together, the two of them set to work on the hard ground. Joe had been brought up on stories about how mean and untrustworthy mountain men were, so Rust's generosity took him by surprise.

Although Joe tried to keep his mind on what lay ahead, memories of home slipped into his thoughts like ghosts. There was Gracie, smiling as she served supper. She had been repeatedly calling to tell him and his pa that the food was ready. He remembered how warm the cabin felt from the stove, and how gloriously it smelled of Gracie's rabbit stew and fresh sourdough. She ladled out stew for each of them and asked them about their day. When Joe confessed he had come home empty handed, she laughed and made a joke about the rabbits being too fast for him. She smiled encouragingly as their pa elaborated on how the present mash was going to be the best ever. Might even sell some bottles to Mulkey in the saloon, he said. She teased him so playfully about making sure he didn't drink them first, that all three of them laughed.

Joe hadn't had any luck with his Sharps for some time, and his traps had stayed empty. If it wasn't for Gracie's housekeeping, eking out the flour, keeping back rabbit bones for the next day's stew, they wouldn't be eating at all. He was so used to her ladling small portions for herself and protesting that she wasn't hungry, that he hardly noticed any more.

Mid-morning, the two riders began the climb up to higher ground. The sun was warm on their faces and the air carried the sharp, fresh scent of pine. The ground was stony underfoot. A mule deer and a couple of pronghorns danced away as they approached. A flock of cranes flew overhead, and their soft whooping cry made the men look up.

'Old Shoshone village ahead,' Rust said. 'When I first came up here, that's where I used to stay. Deserted now. The Shoshone took offence when the trail opened up and wagons started rolling through. Moved higher up into the mountains.'

Joe enjoyed Rust's stories about the old days. The way he described it, life back then was hard but possessed an innocence it had now lost.

'Used to take my pelts and exchange them for

42

food, buffalo meat mostly. Me and the Shoshone braves got along fine. Stayed there one whole winter when the snow was bad. I was a stranger passing through their territory and they offered me shelter. Didn't even have to ask.'

They had come to an incline. Joe's horse slipped on the scree, loose stones scattered down the slope under his hoofs. He waited for Rust to remind him how much better his mule would fare on the high ground.

'They shared their food with me, I gave them what supplies I had,' Rust went on. 'Damn hymn-singers ruined all that. One time, they drove their wagons right through a burial ground. Every time the braves went to try to speak to them, they aimed their rifles at them. Shoshone couldn't figure out what they were frightened of. One spring they decided they'd had enough and moved the whole village.' Rust shook his head. 'Imagine the folks in Backwater taking the place apart and moving miles up the mountain because a band of Shoshone decided to ride through every spring.' He looked over at Joe. 'You're sure going to wish you had my mule when you reach high ground.'

A few miles further on, the trail opened on to a wide plain. The site of the village was spread out in front of them. Ringed by a protective wall of spruce and cleared of scrub, the ground was empty. Shoots of spring grass pushed through the charcoal circles where fires had once been, and the flattened ground where the tepees had stood. Joe's attention kept being drawn to the trees. Something made him uneasy but he couldn't put a finger on it. Rust noticed.

'Feel like you're being watched?'

'I don't know,' Joe said. 'There's something.'

'You are.' Rust chuckled to himself. 'There's wolves in amongst the trees.'

The hairs pricked on the back of Joe's neck. The shadows between the pines were black as pitch. His hand felt for the five-shot in his belt.

'Story goes the Shoshone asked them to guard this place,' Rust said. 'Keep it safe so that one day they can return.'

That evening, as sunset blazed over the mountains, Joe and Rust settled on a place to camp. The ground was stony and the grass was thin. Joe looked around for dry wood to make a fire while Rust hobbled the animals. Never hobbled before, Magic snorted indignantly and raised one foot after the other, which made Rust's work difficult.

'Gonna have trouble with this one when you get in the mountains. Telling you, you should exchange her for Tulip.' Rust sounded as though he was giving Joe good advice. He yanked the hobble tight.

44

The two men laid out their bedrolls each side of the fire and their rifles alongside, Joe's Sharps and Rust's Springfield. Joe used his saddle as a pillow. Rust didn't unload the mule; he took what he needed, coffee pot and pieces of dried buffalo meat for each of them and squatted down beside the fire. The darkness thickened until it surrounded them like a wall. Close by there were mysterious rustlings, sometimes the sound of a footpad. Somewhere off in the distance, wolves howled. At each new sound, Joe peered nervously into the darkness. Rust was oblivious.

'Got to keep an eye out for bears where you're headed,' Rust said. 'Grizzlies all over. One thing you can be sure of, if there's one nearby you may not see him but you can bet your life he's seen you. They terrify a horse, too. I've seen horses rear up and throw their riders at the sight of a bear.'

'That don't worry me,' Joe said. 'A bear came down to the farm once. Me and Pa saw him off.'

'Just need to keep an eye out, that's all I'm saying.' Rust was irritated with him for him not agreeing to trade his horse for the mule.

Mentioning the farm reminded Joe again why he was out here. He should be at home in the barn now, his Sharps on the bench cleaned and oiled, ready for an early start. Some evenings, when the breeze was right, he could even smell Gracie's cooking from where he worked. He would be waiting for her sing-song call that supper was ready. As he pulled the barn door closed after him, so as to hide how untidy it was from her, he would see her smiling from the cabin doorway. He knew that she would have made the cabin spick and span ready for him and his pa. He pushed the thought aside, no point in letting his mind play over that now.

'You come across many grizzlies out here?'

'Grizzlies, black bears, brown bears, wolves, you name it.' Rust stared moodily into the fire. He was trying to frighten him, Joe knew that.

'More coffee?' Joe picked up the pot that had been resting at the edge of the flames.

Rust held out his tin cup and grunted thanks.

'Wrestled a grizzly to the ground once.' Rust couldn't resist. He launched into a story about how, when he was younger, a bear had sprung on him while he sat at a camp fire just like this one. He glanced across at Joe to gauge his reaction. Joe smiled to himself as the story unfolded. It was a hunter's tale about one that got away. Unlikely and exaggerated but told with such conviction, it left Joe almost convinced.

'Got claw marks to prove it.' Rust pulled up the sleeve of his buckskin shirt. A thick white scar ran up his arm. 'On my back there's worse. Lucky to have made it out of there.'

Telling a story about his own heroics cheered Rust up. The fire crackled and spat as the two men took turns in feeding it kindling sticks. Showers of sparks exploded upwards into the night sky. Joe rested on one elbow and listened to Rust's stories get more preposterous as the night wore on. The warmth of the fire felt good on his face. Magic and Tulip watched them from the edge of the circle of orange light.

'One fella you might run into,' Rust said. 'Trapper by the name of Charlie Saltcoat. Trades with the Shoshone like we used to do in the old days, lives up beyond the high plains, hardly ever comes down the mountain.'

'I've heard of him,' Joe said. 'Pa used to bring home stories from the saloon.'

'Been up there on his own so long, he ain't used to people.' Rust was giving a genuine piece of advice. 'Just be careful if you come across him. He don't take to company.'

'Used to be a guide for the wagon trains, didn't he?' Joe prompted.

'That's how he started out. He knows the high passes like the lines on his hand. Came down to town once, years ago, with a pair of women's boots to sell, good ones too, fancy tooling all up the side. 'Course, everyone is interested in a good pair of boots, so folks all kept on at him, where d'you get 'em, Charlie, where d'you get 'em?' Rust paused to feed sticks into the fire, making Joe wait for the rest of the story. He held out his tin mug for a refill. The dry wood cracked like pistol shots.

'Turned out he'd been a-guiding a wagon which had got separated from the train. Belonged to a young couple from back east who didn't have much of a clue about anything, let alone how to drive a wagon through the high passes. Anyhow, snow fell one night and didn't stop. It was all they could do to prevent the wagon getting buried and themselves along with it. They couldn't move forward nor backward. More and more snow fell, day after day. They ended up being cut off for months. This was years ago, turned out to be the worst winter we've ever had.'

Joe shivered. He knew what winters up here could be like.

'Anyhow, the couple ran out of food and froze to death.' Rust went on. 'They'd started out too late in the season, didn't have the right clothes, broke an axle outside Independence, you name it. Charlie had noticed their fancy boots, of course, so after they had passed, he tried to get their boots off. No joy, legs frozen stiff as posts.'

'So how did he get them off?' Joe couldn't resist.

Rust grinned. This story hooked everyone.

48

'Made a fire and had a notion to warm the woman's legs till they thawed and he could pull the boots off. Now, this took a long time. Couldn't lay her too close for fear of singeing the leather. Her legs were frozen so hard, Charlie reckoned it would take days. He got fed up with pussyfooting around, took his bowie and sawed the legs off at the knee.

'You sure about that?' Joe scoffed. This sounded like one of Rust's tall tales.

'You can ask that yard of pump water, Mulkey, if you don't believe me. He was there.' Rust didn't like being interrupted.

'Anyhow, Charlie said he had a pair of men's boots too, outside in his saddlebag. Of course, everyone wanted to see. He led them outside, opened up his saddlebag, and there they were, a pair of fancy, Boston-made, men's boots. Trouble was, they had the feet still in 'em.'

Rust roared with laughter at the look on Joe's face.

Later, Joe built up the fire and the two men settled for the night. When he stared into the flames, his bones aching with tiredness, there was Gracie. She was pleading with him to fix something, the look on her face said she knew he wouldn't get round to it. Rust lay opposite him, hat pulled down, blanket tight around him. Almost immediately, Joe heard his gentle, rhythmic snoring.

The next thing Joe knew, grey light filled the sky, the cold made his teeth chatter and the fire had died. Rust was gone, so was his mule and Joe's horse.

5

Joe threw off his blanket and jumped up. Panic.
Where were they? His heart galloped in his chest.
The freezing air made his bones ache. The
charred ground where last night's fire had been
was stone cold. The prairie grass was trampled
where the animals had stood. The dirt was flattened where Rust had slept.

'Thomas? Hey, Thomas, where are you?' Joe
tried shouting. He cupped his hands round his
mouth and called for his horse 'Magic, come on
Magic. Come on, girl.' She would recognize his
voice.

Back down the slope, the path Joe and Rust had
climbed the previous evening snaked between the
pines. Joe stood still and listened, concentrated on
every sound, desperate to hear the crack of a twig
underfoot, the muffled beat of a hoof, anything.

Long minutes passed while he held his breath. He heard nothing except the sway of the high branches, the thundering of his heart.

Rust wouldn't have backtracked anyway, would he? They had pitched camp in the lee of an outcrop of rock. Joe hurried round the other side. Still nothing. Searching for tracks on the stony ground was futile. There were deer trails between the trees, each one was a path Rust could have taken.

Joe remembered how envious of Magic Rust had seemed. In the end, knowing that Joe would never agree to a trade, he simply stole her in the night. Joe's heart rate slowed. The truth stared him in the face: Rust had planned this. He had lulled Joe with his tall tales while he calculated the best opportunity to unhobble Magic and slip away.

In the west there was yellow light in the sky, grey clouds reflected a sickly dawn. The wind was picking up, a warm, dry breeze dancing down the slopes, snatching handfuls of dust and tossing them in the air. Later in the day, there was going to be a storm.

The only things Joe had left now were his saddle, which he had used as a pillow, the Sharps he had kept beside him all night, and his pa's old five-shot still tucked in his belt. He tried to comfort himself: at least he had his guns. Rust had taken his saddlebags, that meant no food, coffee or canteen. The saddle was too heavy to carry. Joe's anger turned against himself: he should have guessed. How many times did Rust offer to trade his horse yesterday? He should have tied Magic to a tree and slept beside her, not let Rust hobble her. He remembered the indignant look on her face.

Joe heaved the saddle into a stand of spruce and camouflaged it with dead branches. There was no option but to press on. He knew he had to keep heading west, knew that eventually he would come to the high plains and knew that Gold's hideout was somewhere in the mountains beyond. That was where Grace was. He tucked the Sharps under his arm and headed for high ground.

After climbing for a couple of hours, Joe stopped and looked back. His legs burned, lack of breakfast clawed at his belly, and the Sharps was a dead weight under his arm. The wind sang wild, mournful notes amongst the rock faces and gullies higher up the slopes. The ground here was stones and dust; the cottonwoods grew bent double. There was a clear view over mile on mile of the plain below. Joe strained his eyes to try to make out the trail he and Rust had taken the day before, the smoke from a homestead chimney, anything to make him feel less alone. The more he stared, the more he had that feeling again, same as yesterday, a feeling he was being watched. He looked all around him, rocks, trees, clumps of parched grass, nothing else. He remembered Rust's story of the wolves, and held the Sharps tight under his arm.

As Joe rounded an outcrop of rock, he did see something. Way below him on the plain, a line of five wagons headed west. Their canvas bonnets shone in the morning sun. Men and women, tiny specks from up here, strolled beside the oxen, children ran on ahead and then darted back. Joe smiled to himself. Something human, familiar, the sight was like meeting an old friend.

On this side of the rock face, the wind howled. Joe staggered against it. Warm, dusty blasts unsteadied him, knocked him from side to side. Head bowed, he shouldered forward, screwed up his eyes against the clouds of trail dust, and pulled his hat down hard. Every step was an effort. He stumbled. He had to keep looking up to pick his way. Above him, between the gullies and canyons, the pitch of the wind rose to a scream. Its wild, bitter lament played in his ears like a warning. Don't go on, turn back, don't go on. Joe glanced down at the train. Their progress was no faster than his. He remembered the wagons lined up along the town street in Backwater, pictured them queued up at the river crossing. As the wind flung dust in his face, he remembered the exhausted, determined expressions of the emigrants.

The ground was steep. With his free hand, Joe grabbed hold of scrub branches, roots, anything to haul himself up. Keeping hold of the rifle unbalanced him. Underfoot there were loose stones and rock polished by the wind, his boots slipped and slid. The wind punched him like a boxer, body blows, left and right.

At last, the ground levelled, a plateau curved round a sheer rock wall. Joe's heart skipped with relief. His lungs burned, his legs shook. He swapped the Sharps to his other arm. But here, the wind tore down the mountain like a stampede, galloped at him, strong enough to blow him clean over the edge. The gradient he had been climbing had sheltered him, he could hardly stand now.

There were crevices in the wall of rock, some looked big enough for him to take cover. Bent double, Joe struggled across to the nearest one. He dropped to his knees, held the Sharps ahead of him and crawled after it. The gap in the rock face opened into a cave. Until his eyes adjusted, he was blind. The relief from escaping the force of the wind made his limbs feel light. He smiled to himself. This was perfect. He would rest up here until the storm blew itself out.

Then he felt something against his chest. He must have jammed the Sharps against the rock, it was stuck fast. For a second, he thought he must have crawled over some jagged outcrop. But there was no mistaking the cold, hard jab of a rifle barrel against his breastbone. He froze, his heart exploded. A few feet ahead of him in the darkness was a Shoshone brave. He gripped the barrel of Joe's Sharps in one hand and levelled his own musket straight at Joe with the other. Out of the shadows, the man glared at him, fierce, questioning eyes. His face was lean, unsmiling. He was young, Joe's age maybe. A streak of ochre an inch wide ran from his hairline down his nose to his chin. Under his buckskin shirt, his shoulders were muscled and strong. There was uncompromising courage in his hard stare. Joe understood that armed with his Sharps, he was a threat. The brave did not flinch.

As Joe's eyes adjusted, he saw a young woman peering over the man's shoulder. Her hair was tied back, the front of her buckskin shirt was decorated with a zigzag of porcupine quills. She clutched a child tight to her shoulder, a baby swaddled in a blanket. She looked terrified. The man jabbed Joe with his musket. Get out, it meant. Joe wanted to explain that he was no threat, that he just wanted shelter from the wind. He started to say something, tried to force a smile to show them. The man jabbed at him again. Get out.

Joe started to work his way back towards the entrance. Outside the cave, the wind raged. The brave wouldn't let go of the Sharps. Every time Joe pulled at it, the man jabbed the musket into his chest. This was no place for a standoff. With the barrel of the brave's musket inches from his head, expecting him to pull the trigger any second, Joe let go of the rifle. He slid backwards on all fours to the mouth of the cave. The brave kept his musket levelled until Joe was outside.

Immediately the wind pounded Joe like a prize fighter. Above him, amongst the peaks, the moan had turned to a roar. The air was thick with yellow dust. His eyes stung, dirt coated his mouth. Keeping low, he clutched at his hat and hurried round the side of the rock wall. Was the brave following? When he turned, there was no one there.

Out of sight of the entrance to the cave, there was shelter. Two shaggy haired ponies, both with rope hobbles, stood close to the rock wall. They were well fed, healthy and strong, used to hard riding, suited to steep terrain. Joe glanced behind him. Still no one. He ducked down and examined the way the hobbles were tied. He knew he shouldn't risk this. As he looked over his shoulder a third time, the wind screamed.

Just as Joe had his hand on one of the hobbles, he felt cold steel crack into the back of his skull.

The brave stood behind him, aiming Joe's Sharps. Behind the brave stood the woman and child. Joe's blood turned to ice, the warm wind was on his face, but he couldn't feel it. He thought his heart would rupture. He raised his open palms and got slowly to his feet and turned towards them. The brave stared at him, the look in his eye said he had expected this. The woman whispered something and the brave nodded. She stepped forwards with the child tucked under one arm and pulled the five-shot out of Joe's belt.

Joe tried to speak. He wanted to explain, to tell them he meant no harm, that he had been robbed. He wanted to say that he had nothing more than the clothes he stood up in, that he was alone on the mountain. But it was no good. Even if he could have made them understand, it would have seemed like the bunch of excuses it was. They had caught him examining the hobble on one of their ponies. He looked the brave in the eye and waited for him to pull the trigger.

The woman spoke again, abrupt, urgent words in her husband's ear. She stared at Joe as if she were trying to read him, work out what on earth he was doing up here. She held the child close and the five-shot down by her side.

The brave gestured with the Sharps. For a second, Joe failed to understand. The brave swung the rifle towards the pines further down the slope. Go, he meant. Joe didn't hesitate. He scrambled down the slope without looking forward or back. The wind boxed his ears as he stumbled. The soles of his boots slid on the loose stones, spruce saplings whipped at him. He charged helter-skelter for the safety of the tree-line.

Nothing mattered except getting away. Joe tripped, fell, picked himself up and scrambled on. In half an hour he covered as much ground as it had taken him and Rust a whole morning to climb. When he couldn't go any further, he stopped, threw himself down and leaned back against the trunk of a pine, his lungs bursting. He was bruised from falling, his jacket was torn. Trail dust coated the inside of his mouth and hunger clawed at his belly. But there was no one following, he was sure of it.

On his feet and walking now, Joe picked his way down a deer trail. A leaden feeling weighed in his gut: he was headed in the wrong direction. Every step took him further away from Grace. A memory of her filled his head. There she was standing by the stove. It was evening and she had just called him in. He'd had a lazy day. In the morning his traps had been empty so he'd spent the afternoon fishing. No luck there, either. Grace had laughed gently and said it was just as well she'd put by enough leftovers for their supper.

As daylight began to fail, Joe reached the plain. Up ahead, the wagon train had struck camp for the night. Between the wagons he could see the comforting glow of a fire.

6

The smell of woodsmoke and coffee hung on the evening air. Five wagons were circled around a communal fire. A woman wearing a long, grey dress, her hair pulled back under a cotton bonnet, sorted through a pile of firewood and stripped off awkward branches with a hand axe. A second woman, her sleeves rolled up, knelt on the ground and kneaded flour and water in a tin basin. A flour sack and a pail stood beside her. The sounds of voices came from inside the wagons, tired and irritable, on the edge of an argument.

Joe climbed across the tongue of a wagon and entered the circle. Before he could call out, a voice challenged him. Two men stood behind him, both wearing workshirts and cotton pants held at the waist with wide leather belts. They both had straw hats on their heads and full beards. One of them held an old muzzle-loader.

'Come down from the high ground,' Joe started to explain. 'Ain't eaten nor drank all day. Lost my horse, lost my rifle.'

The first man stepped forwards. He was tall, his clothes hung loosely on him. There was authority in the way he greeted Joe. Creases showed at the corners of his eyes as he smiled.

'Welcome.' He gestured towards the fire. 'Come and sit with us.' Joe wondered about his accent – German, Dutch maybe. Gratitude flooded through him, the wagon train meant shelter, warmth and food.

'Caleb, we have talked about this.' Speaking loud enough for Joe to overhear, the man who held the rifle was irritated. It was clear that if it was up to him, Joe would be sent on his way.

'Be quiet now, Ethan.' Caleb didn't look at him. He took Joe's arm and led him towards the fire. The woman had finished kneading and was transferring the dough to a Dutch oven at the edge of the flames.

'You know what we agreed.' Ethan grabbed his friend by the shoulder.

'You agreed, not me,' Caleb snapped. 'Let our visitor sit by the fire and rest.' He signalled to the woman who had been baking to bring Joe a scoop of water. 'Ethan, you have it in you to be a charitable man, so please.' Caleb forced a smile. 'I understand that you are concerned for the welfare of all of us.'

Joe noticed the women turn away. This was an argument they had heard before.

'I won't make no trouble.' Joe felt the warmth from the fire soak into him.

'We turn no one away.' Caleb said. 'Stay and eat with us and we shall give you a bed for the night.'

'There are five families here,' Ethan hissed. 'We do not have food to spare. You know this.'

'We will share what we have,' Caleb said flatly.

'Maybe I can earn my keep,' Joe suggested. 'Help out with whatever needs doing.'

'We need food,' Ethan snapped at him. 'You don't even have a rifle.'

Other people had climbed down from the wagons, attracted by the sound of voices. The women's dresses were threadbare; the men's clothes were patched and worn. Children held their mothers' hands. They all stared at Joe.

'What he eats will come out of my share,' Caleb said.

'You're a fool, Caleb. If we are to survive this journey, we all need every ounce of our strength. You already gave your food away to those others who passed by. If you or any of us falls sick, then someone else has to do an extra share of the work. And now there is no milk because you took it upon yourself to sell the cow.'

'Enough,' Caleb snapped. 'We shall share our food with this stranger tonight, and in the morning, if he offers to help with our chores, we shall gladly accept.'

There was murmuring amongst the crowd of onlookers. Joe couldn't tell if they were in favour of him staying or not.

'I ain't eaten nor drunk all day until this water right here.' Joe gestured to the pail. 'I'd be glad to work for you as payment.'

Discussion continued in the crowd, low, urgent voices. Joe couldn't catch what they were saying.

'None of us have eaten all day.' Ethan was burning up with anger. 'This fool gives away our food to everyone who passes. He takes the word of some farmer who tells him our cow is worthless, and almost gives it to him.'

'The cow was worn out by the journey. There was an opportunity to make some money.' Caleb defended himself. This sounded like a dispute that wouldn't go away. Conversation in the crowd was getting louder, people were taking sides.

'Which others passed by?' Joe tried to change the subject. Caleb was offering him food and shelter.

'A Shoshone brave and his squaw.' Ethan stared at him. 'He gave them our food. Can you believe that?'

'There was a storm.' Caleb appealed to the crowd. 'They had a child with them.'

'He gave our food to a Shoshone child when it was intended for our own.' Ethan opened his hands to show that this was beyond belief. The children in the crowd clung to their mothers' skirts. People were shaking their heads now. Ethan had them on his side.

'I gave them two of strips of dried buffalo meat,' Caleb said. 'Barely enough for a meal.'

'Food that was intended for our own,' Ethan repeated. His face showed that he was holding on to his anger. 'Then there was the trapper. You gave him our coffee.'

'He was alone in the wilderness.' Caleb defended himself again. 'I gave him a few beans in a twist of paper. You all saw.'

'I'll do a day's work tomorrow,' Joe interrupted. 'Sunup till sundown. I don't eat much. I'm grateful to you all for taking me in.'

'My wagon needs fixing,' Ethan said quickly. 'You can work for me.'

From outside the circle of wagons came the sound of wolves howling somewhere in the distance. Everyone's heads turned. One of the women lifted the lid and peered into the Dutch Oven, the smell of baking bread was on the air, burnt but good.

The following day, Joe worked with Ethan. The trees, tongue and yoke of his wagon all needed replacing. Fifty miles back, Ethan had driven across a gopher hole and the wagon had tipped on its side. The repairs he had made had worked loose. There was no spare timber, so the two men spent the morning cutting short pieces from what wood Nathan had picked up along the way, bound and nailed them over the damaged sections.

With such poor material, it was difficult work. Getting the repairs to hold was frustrating and required persistence. Ethan had confidently assured everyone that the job would take him no more than a day, so they had to finish by sundown. Seeing that Joe was better with his hands than he was, Ethan left Joe to it and went off to see to his animals. His two oxen were grazing a short distance off. He also had a mule, which he said was giving him trouble. It was hobbled and munched contentedly on prairie grass when left to itself. However, whenever Ethan approached, it reacted badly, kicked out and ran off a few paces. The worse it reacted, the more Ethan tried to get the creature to do what he wanted. For some reason, he decided that a patch of grass further away was more suitable and tried to tow the confused creature across to it by its horsehair reins. He decided that it must be thirsty, so when the animal refused to drink from the pail he carried over, he lost his temper. When the mule kicked the pail over, he used his whip.

At midday, Ethan brought Joe a glass bottle of water and some strips of jerky.

'How long till you finish?' he said.

That evening Joe joined everyone beside the fire. Some of the men had set traps the previous evening, but the catch was meagre – three skinny rabbits between all of them, scarcely a mouthful each. Joe stared into the flames. Gracie's face danced in front of him for a moment, then disappeared. Wherever she was, it was a long way off.

When the people from the train had done warming themselves by the fire, they started to make their way back to their wagons. The poor meal meant that no one was in the mood for conversation.

'No bread, see that? You had the last of it.' Ethan blamed Joe. 'Flour ran out last night.'

Caleb asked if the repairs were finished.

'Said they would be, didn't I?' Ethan said casually. 'Started at sunup, finished an hour ago.'

'That mule been giving you trouble long?' Joe said. Everyone turned away, they had all heard the beatings that afternoon. They knew what to say to Ethan and what not to say.

'Just got him.' Ethan said. 'Letting him know

who's boss.'

'How long did you say you had him?' Then Joe remembered. Horsehair reins.

'Yesterday. A trapper came by, thought he could scrounge a free meal. Said someone had stolen the saddle for his horse. Didn't have a use for my old saddle so I traded it for the mule.' Convinced that he had come off best from the deal, Ethan was pleased with himself. 'Mule will always come in handy. Save me walking when the trail gets steep, tie her in front of the oxen if the wagon gets stuck.'

There was no point in telling Ethan that he had ridden out here with Rust, Joe reflected. If he told him who Rust's horse really belonged to, it would only lay him open to Ethan's scorn.

'Why? You know anything about who stole his saddle?' Ethan looked at Joe suspiciously. The look on his face meant that he had put two and two together and made five.

Joe remembered Rust whingeing on about trading the mule for his horse. After a hard life-time of carrying Rust and his pelts through the mountains, Tulip was old and tired. But she had walked along quite happily when Rust had her – Joe recalled her slow, swinging gait. Not used to being tied behind a wagon, when the train set off in the morning Tulip would be bound to object and be in for another lashing.

68

'Anyway, I want you to repair the backboard before we start out tomorrow,' Ethan said sharply. 'One corner is rotten. Won't take more than an hour. You'll have time if you begin at first light.'

'A day's work is what we agreed,' Joe said. 'That's what I've done.'

'The work ain't finished.' Ethan stared at him hard.

Joe shrugged. There was one thing he wanted to find out. 'Which direction did that trapper go after he left here?'

'Back up to the mountains.' Ethan looked surprised. 'Why?'

During the night, being careful not to interrupt Ethan's snores, Joe let himself down from the back of the wagon. The cold cut through his jacket, his breath was a cloud in front of his face. Above him the jet-black sky was swathed in a million stars, pinpricks of dazzling light, some as fine as dust. Moonlight reflected off the bonnets of the wagons and the backs of the sleeping oxen. The rocky plain, prairie grass, the pines and the mountain slopes were cast in pewter.

Joe helped himself to the bottle of water and the strip of jerky Ethan had left out for him on the assumption that he was going to carry on with the repairs in the morning. Too big for the pocket of his jacket, Joe slipped the bottle inside his shirt.

The glass was icy cold against his skin. He slipped the knot that tied Tulip's reins to the backboard of the wagon and led her in the direction of the mountains.

Each of Tulip's steady hoofbeats sounded like an earthquake to Joe, a tremor sure to wake someone. In spite of the cold night air, a line of sweat ran down between his shoulder blades inside his shirt. He expected a shout, a shot even. A hundred yards, two hundred – he glanced over his shoulder. There was nothing except stillness and silence, moonlight on the bonnets of the wagons, silver prairie grass, his breath in front of his face.

A mile away across the plain Joe could make out a fire, a dot of orange light in the midst of the darkness. He strained his eyes for the silhouette of a wagon. A lone rider who had built up his fire to last till daylight? Why hadn't he ridden over to spend the night with the train?

As a wash of grey light spread across the sky, Joe entered the foothills. His head was dizzy with tiredness – time to see if Tulip would let him ride. He patted the old mule on her neck and whispered in her ear. She stood patiently as he eased himself up on to her back. Dark stripes were matted in her coat.

Behind the peaks, the sky was the colour of blood. Surefooted and slow, Tulip picked her way over the rocky ground. Joe checked behind him. Mile on mile of couch grass and sage brush rippled green and silver in the early breeze and stretched to the mists of the far horizon. A line of smoke climbed up from the circle of wagons – someone had built up the fire for morning coffee. Joe shivered and pulled his jacket tight around him. He looked for a sign of the other fire but there was nothing, no sign of a wagon, no rider. Maybe he had been mistaken, tiredness playing tricks.

An hour later, making her way up a dusty deer track, a zigzag across a slope strewn with boulders, Tulip stopped dead. Joe was slumped forward as he rode, his head nodded, lack of sleep had caught up with him. The abrupt halt jerked him awake. He slipped off Tulip's back, the hairs pricking on the back of his neck, eyes peeled.

A few yards ahead, a prairie rattler lay coiled in the dust, grey-brown, almost indistinguishable from the surface of the track. Sensing the warmth of the mule on the morning air, it raised its head and stared at them, round black eyes as hard as jet. The thick, coiled body loosened slightly. Dark camouflage patches edged in white, tight layered scales, a white throat under its chin. Three feet long, Joe judged, maybe four. He pulled gently on Tulip's bridle to edge her backwards. The rattler's striking distance was half the length of its body.

The mule understood. Trusting Joe, she took an awkward pace back.

Sensing movement, the rattler raised its head further. With a single, slow, continuous movement, it slid its body into a defensive coil, tail up, head up ready to strike. The rattle sounded hard, dry, a warning. Joe pulled the mule away and the snake leaned after them, black tongue flicking.

On the far side of a boulder, Joe turned the mule and found another path. For a moment, he imagined the rattler might follow them. But the path remained empty, the sun had not yet warmed the morning air.

When Joe tried to remount, Tulip would have none of it. She moved away, tossed her head and flicked her tail with irritation. The ground was steep here, loose stones underfoot made the going slow. Joe reached under his shirt for the bottle and took a slug of water. The water tasted mercifully sweet to his dry throat, washed away the trail dust on his lips. He didn't allow himself more than one mouthful and jammed the cork back in tight. Judging it was wiser not to force Tulip for fear of making her refuse to move altogether, he gave her an encouraging pat on her neck, held the reins and strolled along beside her. His thoughts drifted to Magic, she would have let him ride.

By early afternoon, Joe had reached his old

campsite, the place where he had hid his saddle. It was still there, camouflaged by the dry branches. The sight of it reminded him of home, how it used to sit on the side of the stall in the barn. And then Grace was in his head again, calling from the house. When her pa didn't answer, fearing that something had happened, she ran out of the house to his chair behind the barn where he had been sleeping all afternoon, red eye on his breath. Memory of Grace was a stab to his heart.

Joe passed the entrance to the cave where the Shoshone family had taken shelter. Later, from the top of a rise, he watched the wagon train crawl along the trail far below. The bonnets gleamed in the afternoon sunlight, tiny figures walked beside the oxen. He remembered the tense faces of the emigrants round the fire, torn between siding with Caleb or Ethan, low on food, their instinct for open handedness threatened by fear for their own survival. He patted Tulip on the neck. Dry blood still clung to her coat.

The feeling that someone was watching returned again. Joe shaded his eyes. Apart from the train, the plain below was wide open and empty. Up ahead, the slopes were deserted and littered with boulders. He had heard wolves in the night. Was it possible a pack would track him up here? Beside him, Tulip ambled on. Her steady pace never speeded up nor slowed. As far as she was concerned, there was no danger, nothing to worry about. Joe smiled to himself. Up here in the mountains, their roles were reversed, the old mule was reassuring him.

As Joe rounded a turn in the path, a shot rang out. A bullet ricocheted off the boulder beside him, chippings stung his face. Not a bullet, a musket ball. A Springfield, Joe would recognize that sound anywhere. Out of instinct, his hand went to grab the five-shot in his belt. Nothing there. The warm sweat that had dampened his shirt turned to ice. Where had the shot come from? Who was shooting? Joe seized Tulip's bridle, pulled her close. He felt her stiffen, her eyes rolled left and right. Was she going to freeze or bolt?

Joe scanned the line of boulders up ahead. Nothing. He stared back down the trail he had just climbed. Rocks, dry earth, the slope was empty. Where was the shooter? He'd ducked down some-where to reload, that was for sure. Joe stared into the shadows between the rocks, desperate for some tell-tale sign.

Tulip shifted. Fear was building in her, she wanted to run. In the second Joe ducked his head behind hers to whisper reassurance in her ear, there was a second shot and a dull, wet thud as the musket ball hit. Tulip flinched. For a second, Joe thought she had missed her footing. Then she began to lean on him, her legs folding under her. She sank towards him, then collapsed altogether. Joe fell hard, her full weight slammed down on top of him, crushed him against the path. It was like being under rockfall, he couldn't move, couldn't breathe. There was a crack as he fell, a stab in his side as if someone twisted a knife, it felt like he'd broken a rib. The sudden agony winded him, blurred his vision. Gasping for breath, pain spearing his ribs, inch by inch he hauled himself out from underneath the mule's dead weight. A musket ball was lodged in her temple, a neat, dark hole edged with blood. Tulip lay still, her empty eyes stared, all the breath gone out of her.

7

Joe scrambled to his feet, kept low and ran. His side was on fire, his shirt soaked red. The path was steep here, no cover. Heading for boulders at the top of the rise, he still couldn't see where the shots were coming from.

Crouched in a space where two sandstone slabs leaned together, Joe kept his eyes on the line of scrub up ahead. It wouldn't take long to reload, a minute, maybe two. Any second now, he would show himself.

The afternoon sunlight was hard and bright, the sky pale blue and cloudless. Nothing moved. Down the track, Tulip's body lay where she had fallen. The pain in Joe's side winded him. He felt for the wound through his shirt, as if a touch would give him some relief. When he brought his hand away, it was wet with blood. His brain jolted. Had he been shot? He remembered splinters of rock stinging his face. He lifted his jacket. As he pulled his shirt open, broken glass clattered to the ground, his skin was washed red. Cuts criss-crossed his side as if someone had worked on him with a bowie.

No matter. Joe kept his eyes on the boulders at the top of the rise. Doubled up in a space as small as this, his limbs ached. He ignored the pain in his side. It didn't take this long to reload, did it? The minutes stretched. No shot came. Had the shooter lost sight of him? Was he waiting for Joe to show himself? The muscles in Joe's legs stiffened, cramp threatened. If he stayed bent in half much longer, he wouldn't be able to run.

Then he heard it: hoofbeats, some way over the ridge. Irregular, dancing almost, as if the horse was playing up and the rider struggled for control. Joe crawled out from between the boulders. Eyes on the ridge, stooped low, he scuttered up the narrow track.

The minute Joe broke the ridgeline, mile on mile of undulating, grassy plain opened out in front of him, while in the distance towered the snow-capped Windstorm Mountains. A lone rider charged hell for leather away from him. The ground was flat and the going was firm, it should have been an easy gallop. But something was wrong, the horse bucked and twisted. Maybe the saddle was too tight or the bit was put in wrong. The rider kept the animal on a short rein, hacked with his heels and rode hard. At the same time, he fought to stay in control.

Even from this distance, Joe recognized the rider. Thomas Rust hunched forward in the saddle, hammered along to put as much ground between himself and Joe as he could. Out of range of a Sharps, Joe thought. And of course he recognized Magic, clearly in distress. Rust's answer was the whip.

A fall in the land meant that horse and rider temporarily disappeared from Joe's sight. The echoing vacancy of the great plain bore down on him, acre after acre of prairie grass, the empty sky and the mountains. Joe took the strip of jerked meat out of his pocket and allowed himself a bite, a bitter, charred taste, like chewing tree bark. He was grateful for it.

He took off his jacket and shirt and shook out the remains of the broken glass. Amidst a web of cuts, a shard the width of a bowie blade was stuck in his side. As he tried to pull it out, pain exploded and blood streamed. Afraid he might keel over, he sat down on the grass. Sunlight glinted off the fragments scattered beside him. No water. He didn't let himself think about it. He concentrated on picking out smaller shards, trying not to cut his fingers.

Then, strangely, that same feeling of being watched began to eat at Joe's imagination. Somehow he was imagining it, and not imagining it. He found himself wheeling round suddenly, as if to catch someone creeping up on him. He shaded his eyes and scanned the horizon, right and left. Rust was a speck in the distance now. There was no one else.

What about the Shoshone brave? Joe could be within easy range of his own Sharps right now. He stared over his shoulder. Nothing, just the empty line of the ridge. Anyway, the brave had let him go the previous day. What would he want with him now? What about the campfire he had seen as he left the train? Maybe he hadn't seen it, he couldn't be sure. He pushed the thought away. There was no one here, no living soul for miles. Anyway, he couldn't stay here. He had to move.

Getting to his feet and pulling on his shirt and jacket almost doubled Joe over, each movement broke open the cuts. He caught his breath. High above, a vulture wheeled, black wings spread out like sails. From a graceful arc on the thermals, the bird took stock of what was below. It had been quick to spot the dead mule.

Joe limped along. With every step, pain sawed at his side, the weave of his shirt chafed against the open cuts. His throat was parched, the taste of charred buffalo meat dried his mouth. He concentrated on keeping his breathing regular, steady breaths to control the pain.

Afternoon into evening, he kept going. The colours of the mountains deepened as the sun sank behind them. The rocky lower slopes turned from hazy blue to black. Sunlight reflected pink and gold on the snow of the high passes. Down here, even though the ground was flat, Joe got used to the jolt of pain in his side each time he took a step. He fought it, used it to force himself to carry on, concentrated on it to stop himself thinking. The great fear that waited at the back of his mind ready to ambush him was, even if he reached the mountains, how would he know where to find Grace?

Miles away to his left, beyond the rise and fall of the land, a herd of buffalo grazed, dark shapes against the prairie grass. Families of jack rabbits appeared from their burrows now the heat of the day had passed. The air smelled rich with sage. The ground dipped and at once became soft underfoot, a buffalo wallow. Joe hurried down the slope as best he could till he sank up to his knees in black mud, a sickly sweet smell of rotten grass. He cupped his hands and scooped water into his mouth, the colour of rust, the taste of dirt. He almost forgot the blazing pain in his side, his aching limbs. He felt refreshed, stronger. When he had drunk his fill, he splashed his face, filled his hat and joyously tipped the contents over his head. He laughed aloud.

When he looked up, brackish water streaming down his face, someone was standing at the top of the wallow staring at him. The Shoshone woman from the cave, the child cradled in her arms. Joe looked around wildly. Where was the brave? Was a rifle trained on him? Without speaking, the woman made a sign, pinched the tips of her thumb and two fingers together and gestured towards her mouth. Joe knew what it meant. He stumbled through the mud and up the side of the wallow. He sucked in his breath as pain tore at his side.

The woman gestured again, thumb and fingers held together. Then she held out the baby to show him. It was asleep, swaddled tight in its blanket. She tried once more, to make sure he had understood. The same movement, fingers towards her mouth. All the time, she did not take her eyes off Joe. Her face was solemn. She was asking him because there was no one else.

'This is all I got,' Joe said aloud. He smiled at the woman. The child stirred in her arms. He felt in his pocket for the remains of the buffalo meat he had saved and held it out. He put it on the ground in front of him and stepped backwards. Stooping down was awkward, made him grimace and suck in his breath. The woman hurried round the edge of the marshy ground. As the woman hurried to pick up the food, the brave appeared over the edge of the wallow. He held Joe's Sharps under his arm.

Joe pulled out the lining of his pockets to show he had nothing else. Even this small action made him wince. The brave glanced at him and pulled out a broad-bladed hunting knife from his belt. He cut the dried meat into three, tossed one piece back to Joe, gave one to the woman and took a bite out of the third. He watched Joe take a small bite and slip the rest back into his pocket.

They climbed to the top of the wallow. The sky was flushed pink over the mountains now. Evening mist hid the buffalo herd. A few yards off, two ponies stood hobbled. The brave gestured Joe to sit and pointed to his side, gestured to let his wife inspect the wound. Joe pulled up his shirt, the skin was washed with blood. A shard was still bedded in his side, and the constant movement had prevented the cuts from healing. All of them were bleeding. The woman lay the child on the grass beside her and peered closely. The brave edged closer to look.

The woman reached into a bag at her waist and brought out a package of something that looked like crumbled dirt. She held it out for Joe to see.

He sniffed it. Willow. Meanwhile, the brave worked quickly; with the Sharps beside him, he pulled up a handful of dried grass, gathered some dry buffalo chips. Within minutes he had struck a flint and was blowing on an ember, ready to start a fire. The woman fetched a clay pot from a bag slung over her pony, filled it from the wallow and boiled up a willow bark tea.

When Joe had drunk it all, the brave pressed on his shoulder to show he wanted him to lie back. The tea tasted bitter, his limbs felt heavy, there was a dull feeling in his head. Lack of sleep from the night before and tiredness built up over the day washed over him. He felt dizzy. Joe could see the woman mixing up a paste and heating it over the fire. Behind her, the Windstorms towered over them. Then suddenly his side burned as though he had been branded, he cried out, tried to push himself but the brave held him down, one hand in the centre of his chest. Between the thumb and forefinger of his other hand he held up for Joe to see a shard of bloody glass three inches long, curved like a scimitar. The brave was smiling.

After that, the woman pressed a poultice on the wound, hot from the fire, the sweet scent of buck brush. She guided Joe's hand so he held it in place. Weak from his wounds, exhausted from the strain of the day, the tea made him drowsy. The brave and the woman built up the fire and settled down beside it. Joe watched them. The woman fed the baby, the brave cleaned the blade of his hunting knife. Occasionally they glanced over at him and spoke quietly to each other. Somewhere in the far distance, a wolf howled.

8

The next thing Joe knew, someone was shoving him in the back as if they wanted to tip him out of bed. In his dream, Grace leaned over him, shaking him awake, her face sad, pleading. Something was the matter. Then his pa stood there, hacked him in the side with his bootheel. Pain exploded below Joe's ribs where the cuts were.

Joe was awake, freezing cold. Grey light filled the sky. The fire had died, the Shoshone couple had gone. Instead, Magic towered over him, nudged him in the side with her nose, big, heavy, affectionate shoves. She shook her mane, nickered with pleasure, and whistled gently through her nose. It was the most wonderful sound Joe had ever heard.

Magic nudged Joe's shoulder, rubbed her nose in his outstretched palm and snorted, delighted to have found him. Joe slung an arm round her neck and held her close, he rubbed her forehead and patted her flank. The poor beast was weighed down with all Rust's gear, two great iron bear traps clanked together as she moved; there must have been a dozen smaller traps intended for beaver, racoons, even wolves. Leather bags stuffed with months' worth of supplies were tied to the saddle, but the rifle holster was empty. Joe remembered how Rust used to ride, rifle ready across his lap. The saddle had been put on too tight. Joe reached under Magic's belly and loosened it. Then Joe noticed the whip scars that criss-crossed each flank, dry blood matting her coat. The sight sickened him.

Where was Rust? The range of a smooth-bore Springfield was sixty yards. Straining his eyes in the early light, Joe stared at boulder after boulder, examined the scrub, took account of the rise and fall of the land. There was the great empty plain, the mountains, nothing more. Magic must have wandered off while Rust slept.

Joe led the horse down to the wallow where she drank greedily. He untied the traps and heaved them off her back. There was a canteen tied to one of the saddlebags, which Joe topped up with brackish water. He found a strip of dried buffalo meat and chewed on that. As the sky lightened, the sour, burnt taste lifted his spirits.

Magic stood still for Joe to mount up. She flinched as his leg brushed against the whip scars on her side. The foothills were half a day's ride, Joe judged. An opening to a canyon was dead ahead, his route into the mountains.

It felt good to be riding Magic again, to have her familiar, easy gait under him. For a moment, Joe's thoughts strayed towards home, towards Grace. Easy for him to slip into the kind of homesick reverie that comforts a lonesome rider on the trail, he made himself snap out of it. Rust was somewhere up ahead. Even from this distance, he could see that inside the canyon, the gradient rose sharply and the sheer walls narrowed.

Joe rode for an hour. With Magic carrying him and the mountains close, he had a good feeling. He was making progress. He leaned down, patted Magic's neck and whispered encouragement. She snorted an affectionate reply. Still no sign of Rust, maybe he was already in the mountains. After one too many beatings, most likely Magic had simply turned tail and run off.

Once again, the suspicion that someone was watching him crept up on Joe. He studied the horizon left and right, turned and stared over his shoulder, the empty plain, prairie grass moving in the morning breeze, scattered boulders and a pair of vultures wheeling in the distant sky. A trick the imagination plays when there is no one to talk to, he decided. But the feeling wouldn't go away.

An hour passed. Magic's pace was steady, the sun was warm across Joe's shoulders, the scent of spring grass was sweet in the air. Suddenly, Magic swerved, made a sharp sidestep and tossed her head. Something had unnerved her. She seemed to want to make a detour round the scattering of rocks up ahead. As Joe leaned forward to reassure her, he saw what the trouble was. Spread-eagled in the dirt was Thomas Rust. His head lay at an unnatural angle to his body, colour was bleached from his face, his eyes stared, there was a crust of blood on his lips. Joe leapt down from the saddle. No pulse. In the warm morning air, Rust's neck was ice-cold to the touch. He lay where Magic had thrown him, his neck snapped. A few feet away, a leather horsewhip lay on the ground and next to it, Rust's Springfield, its barrel bent and useless. Magic kept watch but refused to come close.

Joe cut away the topsoil with Rust's bowie and lifted out clods of earth with his hands. He arranged the body and spent the next hour collecting stones. There was no wood for a marker so Joe planted the Springfield at the head of the shallow grave. The old rogue would have liked that, Joe thought. He stole from Joe because he expected people to steal from him. He thought Joe was coming after him because he would have gone after Joe if things had been reversed. He had tried to defend himself the only way he knew. Then he had used the whip one too many times and Magic had thrown him. Seeing him lying there, cold and stiff, Joe felt no resentment, no sympathy. There was one last thing though, Joe remembered Rust boasting about the Colt he kept in his boot. When he felt for it, there it was.

Joe piled the earth and stones over the body as neatly as he could, a frail protection in this hostile land. He stood and bowed his head for a moment. Then, with the bowie and the Navy Colt tucked in his belt, he mounted up and continued on towards the mouth of the canyon. The moment he climbed into the saddle, he sensed Magic's relief at being away from the place.

The canyon walls towered above a dry river bed. The place was in shadow, the air was chill. Sandstone boulders, some as big as ranch houses, littered the floor where a glacier had deposited them millennia ago. There wasn't an even patch of ground. Stones, broken rock and pebbles were strewn underfoot. Magic was forced to pick her way, the going was painfully slow. Above the horse and rider, ponderosas and larches struggled to take root. Higher up, jagged lines of strata the colour of ochre decorated the rock face.

Joe dismounted and led Magic by the reins – he couldn't risk her slipping. The clatter of stones under their feet made a strange echo against the canyon walls. Against his better judgement, Joe kept checking behind him. The feeling of being watched was still there. Ridiculous, he told himself. Rust was dead and buried.

Sometime later, Joe stopped to let Magic rest. The carpet of loose stones was treacherous, her hoofs slipped at every step. Joe took off his hat, poured a couple of inches into it from the canteen and held it under Magic's nose, let her lap it gratefully, then took a swig from the canteen himself. Underfoot, the ground was getting steeper, the stony surface continued in the distance as far as he could see. There was no chance of him remounting.

Above the canyon walls, the strip of cornflower sky deepened to cobalt. Down here, the light was dirty grey and the temperature was falling. Wondering how much daylight he had left, Joe patted Magic's neck and heard her gentle snort in reply. Eyes down, he concentrated on picking his way over the stones.

The echo of a shot exploded off the canyon walls and bounced all around them, the sharp report of a Navy Colt. Joe's instinct was to crouch, look up, try to make out where the shot came from. He felt Magic pull on her rein, fright made her want to rear up.

'Who the hell are you?' Fifty yards ahead, a man faced them. The Mississippi rifle at his shoulder was levelled at Joe's chest. A Navy Colt was tucked in his belt.

'Name's Joe Hansen.' Joe raised his hands slow and wide.

'What's your business up here?' The man did not lower the rifle.

A trapper, Joe thought. He was dressed in a similar ragged buckskin shirt and pants to the ones Rust wore, patched and black with dirt. Oddly, his boots looked polished and new. His grey hair fell over his shoulders and his beard hung down over the front of his shirt like a mat. As he squinted down the rifle sight, his aim was as steady as a rock.

'Looking for someone.'

'Toss that Colt.' The man ignored him.

Joe removed the Navy Colt from his belt and threw it to one side. It clattered on the rock.

'Boots,' the man shouted. 'Take 'em off and throw 'em over.'

'Mister. . . .' Joe started to protest.

'Now.' The rifle barrel waved dangerously.

Joe did as he was told. The rock was ice cold

91

under his bare feet. Holding the rifle to his shoulder, the man stooped down, then briefly picked up and examined each boot in turn. Then he lobbed them back to Joe.

'What did you want to see my boots for?' Joe jammed his feet back in.

'You can tell a guy by his boots.' The man had decided that Joe was no longer a threat and lowered his rifle. 'Looks to me like you're up against it.'

He walked over to Joe, the Sharps tucked under his arm, and held out his hand as if an old-fashioned introduction was the proper thing to do. He looked Joe over, took in the state of his clothes, noticed the dark stain on his shirt where his jacket was open. He didn't know what to make of him.

'Charles Saltcoat,' he said. 'Heard of me?'

'Sure have.' Joe remembered Rust's story of Saltcoat sawing the legs off dead pioneers. 'Down in Backwater, they say you're a hell of a trapper.'

'Do they now?' Saltcoat shifted the rifle under his arm. He was suspicious. 'Hear anything about me guiding wagons through the high passes?'

'Nope.' Joe smiled innocently. 'Why? You a guide?'

Magic suddenly caught Saltcoat's attention, and he lost interest in talking about himself.

'What's in them saddlebags?'

'Nothing.' Joe shrugged. 'Trail chow, that's all.'

'Show me.' Saltcoat cradled his rifle, finger ready on the trigger guard.

Joe untied the saddlebags, tipped the contents on the ground and stood back to let Saltcoat see he had nothing to hide. Saltcoat's eyes lighted on the ammunition.

'What's that for? You ain't got a rifle.'

Saltcoat's manner was friendly enough but distrust was never far away.

'Belonged to a guy I was travelling with. Horse threw him and broke his neck.'

'I know who them saddlebags belong to.' Saltcoat took a pace backwards. 'Thomas Rust, ain't it?'

Before Joe could answer, Saltcoat had levelled the rifle at his chest.

'How do I know you didn't just kill him and steal his saddlebags?'

The light in the canyon was failing. Shadows gathered between the rocks. Above them, the strata that had been bright ochre an hour ago was dark. The strip of sky was grey.

'Horse threw him, I told you,' Joe explained. 'He broke his neck down on the plain. Dug his grave and buried him myself.'

'Thomas never had a horse in his life, always rode an old mule.' Saltcoat narrowed his eyes. The barrel of his rifle didn't waver. 'You're a liar, son. I should put a bullet in you right now and leave you for the vultures.'

'It's the truth. . . .' As Joe began the story, his words sounded like an excuse. What do I have that he wants? Joe struggled to think of something. What do I have to bargain with?

'Stole your horse then shot his own mule?' Saltcoat echoed Joe's words. He didn't believe him. 'How do I know you're not just making this up?'

'If I'd have shot him, I'd have taken his rifle, wouldn't I?' Joe was desperate. 'I don't have it. I'm telling you, the barrel was twisted when he fell. I used it to mark his grave.'

'Telling me you left the man's rifle stuck in the ground?' Saltcoat almost laughed.

'Out of respect. I'm telling you the barrel was out of shape.' Suddenly, the story sounded unlikely even to Joe himself.

Saltcoat couldn't keep his eyes off the contents of the saddlebags, the trail food, ammo for the muzzle loader.

'He beat my horse.' Joe was pleading now. He pointed to the stripes down Magic's flank. 'Magic ain't used to that. She would have reared up.'

'Where are his traps?' The rifle shifted slightly in Saltcoat's hands. He was thinking about something.

Could grab the gun, Joe thought. He took an innocent pace forward, making out he was so set on making sure Saltcoat understood, he didn't realize he had moved. One more pace and he could make a dive for the rifle.

'Rust's traps,' Saltcoat gestured with the rifle barrel. He had noticed Joe take a step. 'Always carried a couple of bear traps as well as all the others. What did you do with them?'

'You can have 'em.' Joe saw his opportunity. 'They're yours. A new set of spring traps would come in real handy up here.' He paused to let the thought settle in Saltcoat's mind.'

'Where are they? I said.'

'They're all in fine condition. You can say one thing for your friend Thomas, he looked after his traps.' As long as he held off telling Saltcoat where the traps were, he wouldn't shoot him, Joe thought.

'Where are they?' The conversation was taking a turn and Saltcoat couldn't see where it was headed. 'Telling me you buried them too?'

'If I'd have killed Thomas, I would have taken his traps wouldn't I?' Joe was emphatic. 'They were the most valuable thing he owned.'

It was almost dark now. Joe could barely make out the expression on Saltcoat's face. He wondered if he could make a dash into the shadows before he loosed off a shot.

'Maybe so, maybe not.' Saltcoat steadied the rifle. 'I'm asking you what you did with the traps. Hide 'em somewhere so you could go back for 'em later?'

'Remember Rust's boots?' Joe thought of something else. 'Deer hide, cow hide, I don't know. Better condition than mine.' He peered at Saltcoat to see how he took this news before he went on. 'Stitching all up the back, repairs good and strong. Those boots are worth something.'

'Buffalo hide, Thomas made 'em himself,' Saltcoat said.

'You and me could do a trade,' Joe said suddenly. 'Information.'

'Ain't you full of surprises?' Saltcoat didn't sound convinced. 'What kind of information?'

I've won him round, Joe thought. He sensed Saltcoat's interest at the prospect of a bargain.

'I tell you where the traps and the boots are, you tell me what I want to know.'

'And what might that be?' Saltcoat said. 'I still ain't sure you didn't put a bullet in Thomas.'

There was a noise some way off in the shadows, loose stones shifting underfoot. Saltcoat wheeled round and pointed his rifle into the darkness.

'You bring anyone up here with you?' Saltcoat hissed.

'Probably a deer, racoon maybe,' Joe said. He wasn't sure what he had heard.

The shadows of the canyon were thick around them now. Saltcoat swung the rifle in a steady arc.

'Ain't no deer up here.' Saltcoat kept his voice to a whisper.

'I'm on my own,' Joe insisted. 'The only folks I've seen are the Shoshone and Thomas Rust.'

'Ain't the Shoshone,' Salt said. 'They've got more sense than to go wandering about in the dark. Come on.'

Saltcoat turned and threaded his way between the boulders. He trod lightly, quick hunter's steps, almost silent over the stones. Joe snatched up his Colt and shoved it in his belt. Towing Magic by her reins, he struggled to keep up. The slip and clatter of stones under Magic's hoofs echoed through the darkness. Sometimes Joe stopped to listen, strained to catch a footstep, the clack of stone on stone. But there was nothing, just Magic's breathing. Saltcoat wasn't used to company, Rust had said. The arrival of a stranger had made him jumpy, made him hear things. That was all it was.

Half an hour later, Saltcoat took a narrow track that climbed up from the valley floor. Joe was walking blind now. He could barely make out the shape of Saltcoat's back in front of him. Twice he cannoned into rocks that overhung the path, once he slipped and fell to his knees. He hurried Magic along for fear of losing sight of Saltcoat altogether.

Then, after a steep climb, the ground evened out, some kind of ledge high up off the canyon gutter. It felt wide and empty to Joe after the narrow path. In front of him in the darkness loomed the square shape of a cabin. A horse was tethered outside, and Saltcoat patted her fondly as he passed.

Inside, Saltcoat lit an oil lamp, the yellow glow soaking through the darkness as the wick brightened. The cabin was a single rectangular room with a fire grate. Table, chair, a narrow bed and a pile of logs were all pushed back next to the walls. Saltcoat knelt in front of the grate and started to build a fire. Joe's gaze fixed on the pairs of boots lined up beside the door, and he shivered as he remembered the story. Saltcoat's bowie hung from his belt in a leather sheath.

'Picked up your hand gun.' Saltcoat stared at the Colt in Joe's belt. 'How do I know you didn't kill Thomas?'

'You'll have to trust me,' Joe said. 'We need to make a trade.'

9

As warmth from the fire spread through the cabin, Saltcoat picked up the pan of last night's stew that was ready on the hearth, and balanced it on a trivet over the flames. While he busied himself with the kindling and stirring the stew, he kept the Colt in his belt and his rifle close at hand. Joe offered to go outside and see to the horses – a pail of water and a sack of hay stood just inside the door. He smiled to himself. He was getting closer, he could feel it. He was in the mountains and this was where Gracie was.

'Come and get it,' Saltcoat called as he ladled the watery stew into tin bowls. He offered Joe the use of the only spoon after he'd finished with it, but Joe gratefully mopped the liquid with a couple of Saltcoat's biscuits.

'Appreciate this,' Joe said. 'Mighty kind of you.'

The lumps of meat that bobbed in the stew water were blackened and tough, the beans resting on the bottom of the bowl were old and hard, but the taste of salt and sage made both men devour their portions without looking up.

'About this exchange you wanted.' Saltcoat occupied the only chair while Joe sat on the floor by the grate, his legs stretched out in front of him and leaning back against the cabin wall.

Joe told the story of the auction and how Rowan Gold burst in. The part of the tale that seemed to interest Saltcoat most was how much Joe's pa got for his daughter.

'I would have given more than ten dollars.' Saltcoat gave it a moment's genuine reflection. 'Everyone knows what a skinflint Jehu Cloake is. I tried to sell him some beaver pelts once. Ended up walking away.'

'Everyone's scared of him,' Joe said.

'Townsfolk,' Saltcoat said contemptuously. 'What do you expect?'

Joe moved the conversation on to Gold.

'Built a place further up towards the snowline.' Saltcoat said. 'Felled the timber himself.'

'Rowan Gold snatched my sister. I aim to get her back,' Joe said.

'You really believe that?' Saltcoat looked puzzled. 'What would Gold take her for? He's already got two wives up there, Shoshone squaws. Good cooks, both of 'em. They brought me food like I've never tasted when I was sick last winter.'

Saltcoat tossed another log on the fire. A shower of sparks exploded up the chimney. As the blaze spat and crackled, shadows lurched round the walls. Of course Gold had snatched Gracie, what other explanation could there be? Joe dismissed Saltcoat's doubts out of hand. He wanted the night to be over, wanted to be on the trail. He was so close, he could feel it. Gracie would be thrilled to see him, he would sit her behind him on Magic, take her back to the farm, and life would carry on. He could almost feel her arms round his waist as they rode home.

Saltcoat pulled a cob pipe out of his pocket and thumbed it full. The air was filled with the rich, dark smell of tobacco, the cloud of smoke was blue in the firelight.

'Problem is, you won't get close,' Saltcoat turned to Joe. 'No one's ever been to Gold's place, not even me. There's a turn at the head of the canyon. He'll see you coming and pick you off from there.'

'Maybe I can talk to him ...' Joe felt sick. Did he think he could just knock on the door and collect Grace as if he were calling to take her to the store? In the distance somewhere, a wolf howled. Saltcoat looked up. Outside, the horses shifted.

'Go anywhere near Gold's place and you're a dead man. Can't say I didn't warn you,' Saltcoat said. 'Anyway, I've kept my part of this arrangement. Now you've got something to tell me.'

Joe described where he had buried Rust, and the wallow where he had abandoned the traps. As he listened, Saltcoat slid his bowie out of its sheath, spat on a whetstone and began to massage the blade. Joe's eyes fell on the pairs of boots by the door, lined up like gravestones. Occasionally, Saltcoat held the blade up to the firelight to inspect the edge. When he was done, he wiped it on the sleeve of his buckskin jacket till it shone.

'Know where I got this beauty?' Saltcoat put the bowie away, reached for his rifle and cradled it in his lap. The food in his belly and the prospect of getting his hands on a new set of traps put him in an expansive mood.

Joe shook his head. Saltcoat was going to tell him the story whether he wanted to hear it or not. He stared into the fire and let Saltcoat talk. He saw a vision of Grace in the flames, her long cotton house dress curled round her.

'Mexican War of '46,' Saltcoat said. 'Siege of Fort Texas. Mississippi Rifle they call it, on account of it being issued to us Mississippi volunteers.'

Joe watched Grace appear and disappear.

'Eight hundred of us, regulars and volunteers. Bombardment went on for a hundred and sixty hours straight, twelve pounders, eighteen pounders. Supplies were cut off, we thought our last day had come. Cannon ball took the leg off the officer in charge – he was standing no farther from me than I am from you now.' Saltcoat exhaled a cloud of tobacco smoke. 'Major Brown. They named the fort after him when he passed.'

As Joe stared, Grace's face became twisted, grotesque, a wraith mocking him.

'Anyhow, six days later General Taylor rode up and rescued us.' Saltcoat enjoyed telling the story. 'And that's where I got this beauty.' He patted the rifle which lay across his lap. 'Handsome devil, ain't she? Brass mountings, .54 calibre. Never was a longarm that could shoot as straight.'

Saltcoat puffed contentedly at his pipe. Outside, the horses had settled. The only sound was the spit of the fire.

'Still hear those Mexican guns in my dreams sometimes.' Saltcoat let his hand rest on his rifle. 'Had enough of army life after that. High-tailed it out of there and headed west.'

Saltcoat reached across and threw another log on the fire. He stood up, stretched, and headed for the low wooden bed.

'Sleep where you like,' Saltcoat said. 'Far

corner's out of the draught.' Somewhere outside a wolf howled and another answered, high, lonesome calls in the darkness.

'What are they yowling at?' Saltcoat grumbled. 'Ain't nothing out there.' Joe shifted his saddle into the far corner of the room and unrolled his blanket. He didn't care how hard the floor was. When Saltcoat pinched the wick of the oil lamp, orange firelight and black shadows waltzed across the ceiling.

'Just the three of them in Gold's hideout?' Joe wanted to be sure what he was up against.

'So far as I know,' Saltcoat said. 'Told you, I ain't never been. Gold's got a reputation as a killer, reckon the only reason he leaves me alone is because I keep well away. Tell you one thing, one time I saw the three of them going hunting together. All of 'em had rifles.'

'You ain't seen my sister with them?' Joe had to ask.

'No, I ain't. Shut up now.' Joe heard Saltcoat turn over in his wooden bed. 'I've told you what I know.'

Soon, gentle snores came from Saltcoat's side of the room. Joe lay back. The warmth of the fire relaxed him, the floor was almost comfortable. He took the Navy Colt out of his belt, pushed it under the saddle behind his head and waited for sleep to kidnap him.

Next thing Joe knew, there was grey light filtering in round the cabin door. The air was cold, only one or two embers still glowed in the grate. Outside, the horses were restless. Maybe that was what woke him. It took him a moment for his eyes to focus in the meagre light. Then he realized it was something else.

Saltcoat was kneeling on the floor next to the door, his back to him. Just about to call out to him, Joe realized what the trapper was doing. Joe threw off his blanket, clambered to his feet. The contents of his saddlebags were spread over the floor. Joe saw Saltcoat slip a box of shells for the Colt into his pocket.

'Hey! What the hell?'

Saltcoat turned. Caught red-handed, he was angry.

'You won't be needing any of this.' Saltcoat struggled for an excuse. 'You're a dead man. Soon as Gold catches sight of you, he'll put a bullet in you before you can even say good morning.'

'Put that back. All of it.' He tried to see what else Saltcoat had taken.

'Keep away from me,' Saltcoat yelled.

In the time it took for Joe to cross the cabin, Saltcoat had his bowie in one hand, his Colt in the other. He slashed at Joe, a wild, sudden movement.

The tip of the bowie caught Joe's jacket.

'I'm warning you,' Saltcoat yelled again. He held the knife at arm's length. He lunged forwards.

'Take you're damn horse and get out.' Saltcoat made another lunge. The blade was clean and sharp.

Outside the horses were unnerved. Their hoofs pounded the dirt. Joe ducked out of Saltcoat's reach.

'Let me take my saddle. . . .' Joe began.

A shot from the Colt screamed past his head and thudded into the cabin wall. Joe heard the horses try to rear up. Magic was easily strong enough to break her reins and take off. He threw himself towards the door.

'That's right.' Saltcoat crowed. 'Get out. You won't be coming back, neither.'

'Let me take my saddle and some food.' Joe was through the door now. He held Magic by her bridle. Outside the cabin, the morning air was biting cold.

'I ain't wasting no more food on you!' Saltcoat thumbed back the hammer on his Colt. 'You'll be dead before mid-day.'

He stood in the cabin doorway, his Colt aimed at Joe's chest.

'Now, get. Before I blow your head off.'

When he was out of range, Joe looked back. Saltcoat still watched him from the cabin doorway. His rifle was at his shoulder now. He wanted to make sure Joe didn't have any ideas about turning back.

In the east, the sky lightened, pink, a smear of blood on a bandaged wound. But in the canyon, the shadows between the rocks were still thick, the walls held on to the night's cold.

Half a mile further, Joe rounded a boulder which hid him from the cabin's line of sight. He looped Magic's reins round a scrub branch and patted her flank. A morning's ride to Gold's place, Saltcoat had said. In his mind's eye, Joe pictured Gracie's face, he was so close now.

Joe scrambled up the rock in search of a vantage point which would give him a view back down to Saltcoat's cabin. The wound in his side ached dangerously, threatened to open again. Joe ignored the pain. His saddle would still be in the corner of the cabin. There was a chance Saltcoat had not yet discovered the Navy Colt tucked underneath. Joe knew that very soon Saltcoat wouldn't be able to resist heading out to retrieve the traps. He would have his chance then, he just had to be patient.

Saltcoat had gone back inside. A line of smoke rose from the chimney. Coffee. Joe pictured Saltcoat standing a pot at the edge of the fire while he gloated over the contents of his newly acquired saddlebag.

Joe's unease got the better of him. Why wait? Grace was bound to be desperate to see him. Joe himself had felt homesick on this journey, what must it be like for her? Why should he delay while Saltcoat warmed himself by his fire? He could rush the cabin, burst in, snatch the saddle and be out of there before Saltcoat realized what had hit him. If he grabbed his Colt, then Saltcoat would be sure not to follow. Joe convinced himself he could do it in under a minute.

With Magic tethered out of sight of the cabin, Joe kept close to the rock face and worked his way back down the canyon. He trod lightly over the loose stones. Every few yards he crouched down and waited. He half expected Saltcoat to appear in the doorway. But there was no sound, no movement from inside. When he reached a boulder directly opposite the cabin door, he ducked down, eyes peeled. The door stayed shut, a wisp of smoke rose above the chimney. Twenty yards, no more. Joe couldn't wait any longer.

Keeping low, Joe hurried across the open ground, quick, light steps. He leapt at the door, booted it open, practically took it off its hinges. With a wild, screaming yell, he threw himself inside. Saltcoat was standing at the table, his back to him. Joe's saddlebags were beside him, the contents spread out for examination. Saltcoat turned, reeled back upending the table, scattering Joe's belongings, his shocked face white, eyes staring. His mouth moved but no words came out.

The saddle was no longer in the corner. Where was his Colt? Joe was frantic. Saltcoat pulled himself upright, started to say something. There it was, on the floor at Saltcoat's feet. It had been on the table with the contents of the saddlebags. Joe made a dive, shouldered Saltcoat in the gut so he fell backwards and crashed into the upended table. Joe scooped up the Colt, the saddlebags. There was the saddle, by the grate. Saltcoat was shouting now, reaching for his precious rifle. He had propped it against the wall after he finished singing its praises the night before. 'You damn son-of-a-gun. What do you think you're doing?' Joe snatched up the saddle by the horn and swung it wildly at Saltcoat.

Joe made it to the door. Out of the corner of his eye, he saw Saltcoat had the rifle in his hands. He ran till his lungs burst, Colt in one hand, saddlebags flapping over his arm, hauling the saddle along with the other hand. Stones slipped and scattered under his feet. He glanced over his shoulder, half expecting Saltcoat to be chasing after him. But no. He was leaning in the cabin doorway, rifle raised to his shoulder, squinting along the sights, taking his time. Joe zig-zagged. Five paces right, three left. Odd numbers, different each time. He kept his head low. Up ahead was the boulder which hid Magic.

Then the shot came. The ricochet whined off the canyon wall. The echo bounced away down the canyon. He turned. Saltcoat was already reloading. Joe had to get out of range. He started to zig-zag again. Exhausted now, his legs would hardly keep going. The gash in his side had opened, he couldn't let the pain slow him. He dragged the saddle, the soles of his boots slipped on the loose stones.

Ten yards. Magic was behind the boulder. He knew Saltcoat would be taking aim. One last zig-zag. When the shot came, Joe was beside the boulder. It felt like a branding iron had been driven into his thigh. He slammed face down on to the rocky canyon floor as though someone had kicked his legs away. Saddle, saddle bags flew out of his hand, the Colt skittered across the stones.

The world spun. For a moment, Joe lay there dazed. Then, expecting a third shot at any second, he hauled himself along on his belly to the safety of the boulder. Pain blurred his vision, stones tore at his chest and stabbed into his good knee. He dragged his wounded leg behind him like a carcase.

'I'll let you bleed out, then I'll come for you. Hear me?' Saltcoat's jeering words echoed down the canyon. 'You're a dead man. Ain't wasting no more ammo on you.'

Joe's head swam. He made a grab for the Colt and heaved the saddle behind the boulder. Blood soaked the left leg of his pants. The pain knocked the breath out of him. Magic understood. She leaned down and gave him a gentle nudge.

For the moment, Joe couldn't tell whether or not the shot had broken his leg. His hand shook as he took his bowie and cut away in the fabric of his pants. His thigh was slippery and red. The wound, a dark circle the size of a dime, pulsed blood. The lead ball was still in there. The pain burned like fire, tore the breath out of his lungs. Worse than that, in his head, the nightmare thought came, he'd never make it to Gracie now.

Joe undid his belt and wrapped it round his leg above the wound and jerked it tight. He moaned to himself, rolled on to his side in an attempt to hold the pressure. Let you bleed out, then I'll come, Saltcoat had said. Pulling on the tourniquet sapped Joe's strength. He lay back, felt his consciousness slide. Easy to slip away now, it would be like falling asleep. His leg was a crucible, burning up. He wanted it to be over. Then he felt a shove on his shoulder. Magic nudged him, kept him awake.

Joe had let go the pressure, the belt had slipped, the tourniquet was useless. Fresh blood shone on the stony ground. One last effort. Joe sat up, fought through the pain and hauled the noose tight, tighter than before, tighter than he could stand until the flow of blood stopped. He knotted the belt, picked up his Colt and slumped back against the rock. Pain caged his wound, the belt scored his leg, his whole body was racked. His vision blurred. Sometimes he was aware of what was around him, sometimes he wasn't, Magic standing close by, the rock he leant against, the canyon floor, the lightening sky, the breeze on his face. How long he had been there, minutes, hours, he didn't know.

Once he thought he heard gunfire, a shot from a muzzleloader followed by the crack and whine of a Colt. He couldn't be sure. It could have been a memory, a dream, something he imagined. Gracie stood in front of him. She was waiting for him, he stretched out his arms but he couldn't reach her. He was too close to a fire, his body was burning up. His shirt was soaked. Blood, sweat, he didn't know. 'Ain't wasting no more ammo on you.' Saltcoat's prophesy rang in his head. 'You're a dead man.'

10

'What happened to you?' The voice was far off, a call from somewhere. It sounded familiar, but Joe couldn't say who it was. At first, he thought it was his imagination playing a trick.

Something nudged him in the ribs. Magic. Joe started to remember. He struggled to open his eyes. He was cold. Icy cold. The weather must have changed. His whole body shivered. He could hear his teeth chatter in his head. There was someone there, someone leaning over him.

'Hell, you look more dead than alive.' It was a man's voice, someone Joe knew. The sun was behind him, his face was in shadow.

'Hey.' That nudge in the ribs again, sharper this time. It wasn't Magic, he could see the horse standing some way back. The man prodded him with the toe of his boot, a tentative prod at first, just to wake him, then harder.

'That trapper do this?' The man stared at Joe's leg.

Joe couldn't answer, his throat was as dry as paper.

'Looks like it hurts some.' The man shoved Joe's thigh with his bootheel. A branding iron seared his flesh, a dry, strangled cry came from somewhere deep inside him. The man laughed. 'I can tell you, that trapper won't be shooting you no more.'

Jehu Cloake. Joe remembered. Things started to fall into place. The smoke from a campfire down on the plain, the feeling someone was watching him. Cloake had tracked him all the way.

'So, she's up here. You brung me right to her.' Cloake laughed at his own cleverness. 'Guess I should be grateful.'

With his boot pressed on Joe's thigh, Cloake reached down, slid the Colt out of Joe's hand and tossed it aside. It was all Joe could do not to scream for him to stop.

'Your pa never was any good. He had his chance just like the rest of us. What did he do with it? Threw it away.' Cloake stared down at Joe, his thumbs tucked in his belt. 'And now look at you. Rode all the way up here just to get yourself shot. Apple don't fall far from the tree.'

'She'll never go with you.' Joe's voice scratched

at his throat, Cloake had to lean closer to catch what he said. 'You're wasting your time.'

'She's mine, bought and paid for,' Cloake sneered. 'A deal's a deal. Odds on Gold is sick of her already. Probably pay me to take her off his hands.'

'You don't know what you're talking about. Gold will shoot you on sight.' Joe tried to come back at him, but his voice was weak. Cloake's boot still pressed on his thigh.

'Hell, he will.' Cloake slipped his hand into his vest pocket and produced a fat roll of bills. He waved it in Joe's face. 'See this? No one says no to this, least of all Rowan Gold. Think he'd be living out here in the back of nowhere if he had this kind of money? You're just like your pa, you don't get how the world works. You rode up here with nothing. I came to make a deal, make an offer, a real offer, not ten bucks like I gave your old man.'

Cloake tucked the roll back into his vest pocket. 'Point is, for that kind of money, he'll sit down to talk. It's you he'd shoot on sight, not me. If he turns me down, I'll shoot him and take the girl anyway. You heard the story about how my wife ran off. Think I'm going to let some woman give me the slip a second time?'

'Don't matter,' Joe's voice was little more than a whisper, breathless with pain. 'Gold or no Gold,

115

Gracie won't go anywhere with you.'

Even if he could hear him, Cloake wasn't listening.

'Made yourself a tourniquet?' Cloake leaned down and tugged at the knot. 'Worried you'd bleed out?'

Pain erupted again. Joe choked back the desire to yell, forced himself upright and made a grab for Cloake's arm. Cloake shoved him away and continued pulling at the knot. When the belt came loose, Joe's leg was wrapped in flame.

'Slug still in there,' Cloake said. He flung the belt far out into the canyon where it lay like a shed snakeskin, no good to anyone.

Cloake pulled himself upright and gave Joe's leg one last kick for good measure.

'Overheard that trapper say he'd let you bleed out.' Cloake laughed. 'Looks to me like you almost have.'

Cloake hauled himself up on to his horse. He yanked the reins, kicked his heels and didn't look back. In a second, he was round the boulder and out of sight. Joe listened to the echo of hoofbeats getting farther and farther away.

Joe fought the pain. If he gave in, it would overwhelm him, he knew that. It would be easy to let himself slip back into unconsciousness, it would be a relief. Instead, he forced himself to focus. If

Cloake did get Gracie, he could ambush them on their way back. They would have to pass by here. He could crawl across the stones, grab his Colt and lie in wait.

Or maybe, Gold would shoot Cloake. A turn at the head of the canyon, he'll see you coming and pick you off from there, Saltcoat had said. If Joe could trail Cloake up there, he would have the advantage of surprise. Gold wouldn't be expecting Joe to show up right on Cloake's heels. Maybe Cloake had done him a favour after all. Just for a second, he believed everything was going to go right.

Then Joe looked down at his leg. Cloake had made sure he opened up the wound again, his pants were soaked with blood. An ambush, following Cloake up to Gold's hideout, was pie in the sky. He was in pain, too weak to climb into the saddle. He hadn't even got the strength to crawl out into the canyon to fetch his belt.

Yes, he had. Ten yards to his Colt, twenty to the belt. Joe started to haul himself along on his back. His good leg pushed, his elbows pulled. Hard going, the stones snagged his clothes, his wounded leg dragged, each movement tore his wound open a little more. A wave of pain threatened to drown him. No choice but to head into it. Each shove, each pull hardly gained him a foot of ground, inches sometimes.

Hoofbeats. Out from behind the boulder, Joe was spread-eagled on the canyon floor, a rabbit in a rifle sight. Whoever it was was getting closer, taking their time. Joe screwed up his eyes. The echo meant he could hardly tell which direction the hoofbeats came from. Then he knew.

'Having trouble there?' A voice called out to him, a menacing voice making a neighbourly remark. The rider rode right up to him till the horse's front legs were inches from Joe's face. Cloake climbed out of the saddle, his boots hit the ground with a thud. 'That leg of yours looks terrible. You're gonna bleed out, son.'

Cloake strolled across to where he had tossed the belt. For a moment, as he stooped to pick it up, Joe imagined he was going to hand it over to him. Then he crossed to where he had kicked the Colt. He tucked the handgun in his waistband, coiled the belt and shoved it in his pocket.

'Just thought you might be getting ideas,' Cloake said. 'I came back to tidy up. You won't be needing this.' He patted his jacket pocket. Joe's eyes fell on his knuckles where the fingers were missing.

Joe tried to say something, but the words cracked in in his throat. Under the brim of his hat, Cloake's face was in shadow. He would be grinning at him, Joe knew that. 'Anything you want to say to me before I head off to get what's mine?' He was waiting for Joe to beg, but Joe wouldn't give him the satisfaction.

Cloake mounted up and turned his horse. Joe lay back on the stony ground and listened to the hoofbeats recede. He felt cold again. His shirt was wet with sweat, but he shivered. The longer he lay still, the more the pain in his leg receded to a dull ache, the slightest movement made the pain explode. As he lay there, the canyon walls swayed round him. He thought of Gracie. When they found his body, at least she would know he had come for her, he hadn't abandoned her. That was something.

Staring up at the strip of sky, Joe imagined noises. Gunfire further up the canyon, the dull explosion of a muzzleloader, the crack of a handgun, voices calling, though he couldn't make out the words, he could have been dreaming.

Faces appeared and disappeared in front of his eyes, Joe's pa stared out across the plain, Gracie smiled, Rust held his rifle. Joe's sense of time disappeared, how long had he lain there? An hour, two, how could he tell? When he opened his eyes, the mountain peaks were blurred above him; when he closed them, faces danced against a background of fire, Mulkey looked sad, Saltcoat took aim from his cabin door. Pretty soon Joe wouldn't have the strength to move at all.

Then he felt himself float. Quite suddenly, Joe felt his body lift off the ground and sway in the empty air. His leg still burned but this sensation made him smile. He opened his eyes, someone was carrying him. Two people. One held him under the shoulders, the other by the ankles. Shoshone braves. No, Shoshone women, one with a Colt shoved in her belt, the other had propped her rifle against a rock. They carried him easily back into the shade behind the boulder where he had lain before. Magic still stood there. They set him down carefully.

One of the women picked up the rifle and held it ready. She was shorter than Grace, Joe judged. Dressed in a buckskin shirt and pants, her dark hair was tied in a plait, her face was solemn. She studied Joe with an unflinching stare, she didn't trust him.

The woman with the Colt was in charge. Dark hair tied back, she wore similar buckskin clothes, but hers were decorated with bright-coloured beads in geometric patterns. She smiled at Joe and genuine sympathy showed in her eyes. While her friend with the rifle stood guard, she examined his leg.

Joe watched the women with interest. He felt

distant from everything, an observer, as though this was happening to somebody else. The woman set down the rifle, gathered handfuls of dry grass and struck a flint to start a fire. The other woman slipped something under his leg and he felt a tourniquet bite into his thigh like wire. He watched both women peer at his wound and then stare at his face as if they were trying to decide something. He listened to them talk to each other, abrupt, precise phrases which communicated exactly what they meant to say, none of which he understood. One of them lifted his head while the other held a canteen to his lips, cold, spring water. It tasted like paradise.

As the women stared down at him, Joe tried to thank them for the water. The words jammed in his throat, he couldn't get them out. Then one of them held up a stick in front of his eyes to show him and rammed it crossways into his mouth. Joe wanted to spit it out but she pushed his jaw up to hold it in place. She nodded when she thought Joe understood. He could smell the smoke from the fire, burning sage leaves. Then he smelled burning flesh. A blade probed the wound in his leg, white hot. An arc of pain curled through his body. On his tongue, he tasted the sap from the stick, acerbic and sour. When he tried to sit up, to reach down to his leg, one of the women held him down.

A second later, the woman with the Colt held something in front of his face. Joe struggled to focus. She grinned at him. A bloody musket ball was pinched between her forefinger and thumb.

The woman who had held the rifle went to work on a poultice, the other found the scars under his shirt. They dealt with cleaning his old wound and healing his new one. They gave him bitter tea to drink, the acrid taste of bark. The blazing pain in his leg retreated to a dull ache.

The next time Joe woke, he was alone, sunlight filled the canyon, the shadows had retreated into the crevices between the rocks. Hunger clawed at his belly and his throat was parched. His leg was tightly bound with strips of hide, the bleeding had stopped, the pain had lessened. Magic stood patiently beside him.

When the shadows lengthened again, the women returned. Joe was relieved to see them. He felt light-headed and wanted to talk.

'Come looking for my sister,' Joe began. 'Gracie. Grace Hansen.' He pronounced the name slowly, emphasized each syllable.

The women ignored him. A jolt of pain stabbed his thigh as they undid the binding to inspect the wound.

'Gracie,' Joe said. 'You come across anyone by that name?'

The women concentrated on staring at his leg. One of them undid a small leather purse from her belt and shook a pile of dry herbs into her hand. The other tipped in a little water from her canteen. Joe watched her massage her hands together to make a paste.

'Hey,' Joe raised his voice. 'Grace. You know where she is?'

One of the women pressed the herbs directly on his wound and smoothed it flat. Even this slight pressure made Joe gasp. He snatched at the sleeve of the woman nearest him. She glared at him and pulled away.

'Grace,' Joe repeated. 'My sister. I'm looking for her.'

The women started to bind his leg again. He could feel the cold poultice against his skin. He was afraid they would bandage him up and just ride away again. Grace was up here somewhere. Surely one of them would recognize her name. He tried again, louder, slowly articulating each syllable, Grac-ie Han-sen. He added a pantomime of gestures. He pointed at each of them for woman, tapped his cheek to show the colour of Grace's skin, patting his chest with the flat of his hand to show how fond he was of her. The women watched carefully.

'Grace.' Joe said. 'Grace.'

One of the women said something and the other replied, surely they recognized the name. They continued to watch him with interest, so Joe thought he must be getting somewhere.

'Joe.' He pointed at his chest and smiled warmly. 'Looking for sister, Grace.'

He waved his arm vaguely in the direction he'd been travelling.

'Joe.' The woman with the beads rolled the unfamiliar sound in her mouth. 'Kimana.' She smiled and tapped her breastbone. Then she pointed at her friend: 'Chepi.'

'Gold, you know him?' Joe tried a different tack. 'Rowan Gold.'

A look crossed Kimana's face, her eyes narrowed a fraction, Joe was certain he saw it. Chepi was impassive.

'On the way here, I was robbed.' Joe started to gabble. Talking at half speed frustrated him. 'I don't know how you came by it, but that's my handgun.' He leaned forward and touched the Colt in Chepi's belt, just the tip of his fingers to illustrate what he meant.

The atmosphere froze. What had been puzzlement and polite curiosity on the part of the women switched to icy distrust. They leapt to their feet. Kimana snatched the Colt out of her belt, Chepi made a grab for the rifle. They spoke urgently to each other, words tumbling out fast, some kind of argument.

'No, no.' Joe raised his hands above his head, palms outward. 'I didn't mean anything.'

Chepi jabbed him in the ribs with her rifle. She shouted. She was ordering Joe to do something, it took him a moment to work out what it was. She nodded towards Magic.

'I can't ride,' Joe said. 'I can't mount up.'

Kimana shouted now. The Colt was steady in her hand. Joe used the boulder behind him and levered himself to his feet. Pain erupted in his leg again. Both women took a pace back, out of reach in case he lunged at them.

'Please,' Joe said. 'I didn't mean anything, I wasn't going for her gun. I've just come for my sister, Grace.'

There it was again. A look between them, a hint of recognition at the sound of Grace's name. They knew where she was, Joe was certain of it.

Another jab in the ribs with Chepi's rifle. Kimana waved Joe to hurry up. He leaned against the boulder, put his foot in the stirrup, leaned forwards and hauled his bad leg over the saddle. Holding Magic's reins, Kimana mounted her own pony. Chepi poked him in the back with the rifle to remind him she was still there.

The three riders made their way up the canyon,

Magic between the two Indian ponies. Joe gripped his saddle with both hands to stop himself falling. Every one of Magic's steps was a dagger twisting in his thigh. The light was failing, grey and dusty. Pitch black shadows clung to the base of the rocks and filled the crevices in the canyon wall. Above them, the sky darkened. Joe pulled his jacket round him.

Four, five miles, Joe reckoned. Above him was a strip of stars in a black sky. Even with darkness lying thick in the canyon, the riders kept up the same steady pace.

The ponies knew the way. Joe felt his strength ebb. His leg burned, his head swam, he was weak. He felt his grip on the horn loosen, he swayed in the saddle. Each time he was likely to fall, a jab in the back from Chepi's rifle brought him to.

Eventually, the three of them turned off the trail. Kimana's pony climbed up a narrow track between two boulders. A narrow entrance between the rocks before the land flattens out, Joe remembered Saltcoat's description. The ground underfoot had been levelled, some kind of yard, maybe. Through the darkness he could just make out the shape of a building. A dig in the back meant dismount; Kimana helped him. He knew the rifle was still trained on him.

Hay and horses. Joe smelled the barn as Kimana

pulled open the door. In a stall somewhere, a horse stirred. It was pitch black inside except for glimpses of stars through cracks in the roof. Kimana led him over beside one wall and pushed him gently down on to a pile of hay. She said something and took him by the wrist. Chepi's rifle barrel pressed against his ribs.

Before he realized what was happening, Joe felt his wrist being tied. When he tried to move, he found he was lashed to a hitching post. The rope chafed his skin, tight enough to remind him that he was going nowhere. His leg burned, exhaustion weighed him down. But he didn't care, a tide of joy swept through him. So what if he was tied up? He was alive; Grace was here somewhere. He had made it. As he heard the barn door being pulled shut, he sank back gratefully into the hay.

11

The sound of a struggle came from the darkness on the other side of the barn. Men wrestling or someone held down, fighting to escape, grunts, cries muffled so you couldn't make out the words. Was there a trap door, some kind of cellar? Was a man imprisoned down there? Joe had been dead asleep. Being suddenly jerked awake filled him with fear, sweat ran down inside his shirt. He struggled to sit up, his leg burned, the rope bit into his wrist.

An animal caught in a trap, maybe that was it. Whoever or whatever it was thrashed in the straw, kicked and butted against the wooden wall, made the whole barn shake. The noise unsettled the horses. Somewhere back in the shadows, they shifted and stamped, three of them, four maybe.

When one of them whinnied more out of puzzlement than alarm, the disturbance stopped. Whatever it was, whoever it was froze, listening.

'Who's there?' Joe made his voice sound angry.

Silence.

'I said, who's there?' Joe tried again.

Whoever it was, whatever it was, listened. Joe could feel it. The thrashing around started again, the fear and fury of a pony at a rodeo.

'Can't you talk?' There was no cellar. Joe worked it out. Somewhere on the other side of the barn, someone was tied up and gagged.

Muffled cries. More kicking against the floor. Someone was trying to communicate with him.

'I'm tied up,' Joe called. 'Can't get to you.' He lay back again.

Across the barn, the sound of struggle continued. Who was this guy? Had the two Shoshone women captured him, too? What was this place, anyway? When they brought him here, he'd assumed he'd arrived at Gold's hideout. Now he wasn't so sure. If it was Gold's place, where was Gold?

The darkness in the barn was absolute. The cracks in the roof allowed Joe to glimpse the stars, but didn't let in starlight. With the rope cutting into his wrist, he took stock. The barn was looked after, the hay smelled fresh, recently turned; the horses seemed content, which meant they had been fed. Lying still on the hay allowed the pain in his leg to subside.

Joe's imagination drifted. He remembered the barn at home, and how he loved hiding away out there, away from Pa, away from farm chores, away from everything. But it was always a mess. The only place that was ever neat and tidy was the work-bench where he saw to his Sharps. He remembered Grace calling out sing-song reminders from the house. 'Used that broom I left out for you, Joe?' He ignored her. She would call out to him two, three days running, more maybe. Then, after an enjoyable trip to the river, he would come home and find the barn swept and tidy. Grace had spent the day in there clearing up after him.

Someone had hold of his shoulder and shook him. Joe took a swing with his free arm, tried to cry out, but there was a hand over his mouth.

'Don't yell, understand?' The voice was a hoarse whisper.

It was Cloake. His heavy body pressed on Joe, his foul breath was in his face.

'Those two squaws bring you in?' Cloake lifted his hand off Joe's mouth. 'They jumped me from behind, a way up the canyon from where I left you. Didn't give me a chance.'

'Was that you, making all that noise?' Joe shoved him off.

'Keep your voice down,' Cloake hissed. 'They tied me to a hitching post, but I got free. Found this nail on the floor, managed to wear the rope away. Taken me all night.'

'This Gold's place?' Cloake was the last person Joe wanted to talk to, but he had to know. 'Is Gracie here?'

'Think those squaws could build a barn like this by themselves?' Cloake pressed a horseshoe nail into Joe's hand. 'I ain't seen Grace yet. Get yourself free with this. Next time they come in here we'll jump 'em.'

'You left me to bleed out,' Joe said.

'They're going to shoot both of us.' Cloake was adamant. 'They didn't do it yesterday so they'll do it in the morning. We're on the same side now.'

'Hell we are.' Joe pulled away from him. He could feel Cloake's great bulk beside him in the darkness.

'Gave you the nail, didn't I?' Joe remembered Cloake waving the roll of bills in his face. This was him attempting to make a deal. 'You'll get yourself free because of me.'

'Those Shoshone women saved my life. If they hadn't come along, I'd be dead after what you did.'

'If they're so fond of you, why did they truss you up?' Cloake laughed. 'They're picking their time, that's all. Just get yourself free. When they come in in the morning, you take one, I'll rush the other.'

'What about Gracie?' Joe didn't trust Cloake any further than he could spit, but something niggled: why had the women tied him up?

'If Grace is here, we'll find her. She could be tied up somewhere, too.'

Joe hadn't thought of that. He'd imagined Grace waiting to see him, not held prisoner.

'When we find her, she comes home with me,' Joe said.

'I ain't getting into all that now,' Cloake sounded irritated. 'Just get that rope off yourself. All I know is Grace is up here somewhere. Those squaws took my gun and my money. I ain't letting 'em get away with that.'

Cloake said something about getting some shuteye, Joe should wake him when he was done. Joe wasn't listening. A vision of Grace tied up and in pain somewhere filled his imagination. He picked at the rope with the nail, strand by strand – this would be a long job. The rope was woven tight and spliced together, as strong as iron. Now and then the nail slipped and stabbed him in the wrist, but he didn't stop. Grace was close by. Soon he heard Cloake's snores from the other side of the barn.

The sound of the barn door being pushed open jolted Joe awake. Early daylight showed through the cracks in the roof. He still held the nail in his hand. The rope round his wrist was more than half picked away, but still held fast. Across the barn, Cloake was sitting upright watching him, back to a pillar, arms behind him and gag in place round his mouth just like the women had left him. There was something Joe hadn't been able to see during the night. Cloake had a purple swelling over one eye the size of a plum, and the eye was part closed.

Chepi stayed back by the door, rifle at her hip, and covered both the men, while Kimana came towards Joe with a canteen of water in her hand. She knelt down and started to undo the strips of hide wrapped round his thigh. With the tight bandage removed, his leg felt light. He saw Cloake staring at him, waiting for him to make the first move. By the door, Chepi relaxed, tucked the rifle under her arm. Cloake signalled, a nod towards Chepi for Joe to see. He glared at him. Joe shook his head, still tied up he meant. Cloake glared again: come on.

Kimana peered at the wound on Joe's thigh, no infection, the blood had dried and it had started to heal. She shook some dry herbs from the leather bag at her waist into her palm, moistened them with water from the canteen, and pressed them lightly over the wound. She worked quickly and carefully, wrapped the leg again, not so tight this time. Now, Cloake signalled. Do it now. He stared at Chepi by the door, I'll take her. He was wild-eyed. What are you waiting for?

Her work finished, Kimana looked up at Joe. That was when she noticed the cuts on his wrist, saw the half-severed rope. She shouted out, grabbed Joe by his free hand and twisted his wrist; the nail dropped on to the floor. She grabbed it and in a single fluid motion, swung back her arm and gave Joe a stinging slap across the face. She yelled, pointing at him, stabbed at the bandage with her finger. I take a slug out of your leg and this is how you repay me? Joe got the gist.

Out of the corner of his eye, Joe could see Cloake start to move. Didn't he realize Joe was still tied to the post? Rifle in hand, Chepi ran towards Joe, she wanted to see what the yelling was about. She saw the scratches on Joe's arm. Kimana showed her the nail. When she pulled at the half-severed rope, she laughed. You thought you could escape from us, well, you can't. She stuck the rifle barrel into Joe's gut, held it there and glared at him, eyes blazing. Just give me an excuse. Joe saw her finger slip off the trigger guard.

Kimana said something and snatched up the canteen before Joe had a chance to take a drink.

After a moment, Chepi lifted the rifle away. She raised the butt and motioned bringing it crashing down on Joe's jaw, as if nothing would give her greater pleasure.

Across the barn, Cloake was wild with fury. Joe could see it. What's the matter with you? Why haven't you made a move? Coward. He mouthed the word deliberately so Joe could see. The two Shoshone women turned their back on Joe and made their way over to Cloake, who sat as if he were tied, hands behind him, gag over his mouth.

'Don't do nothing,' Joe called out. He saw what Cloake was going to try. 'If they wanted us dead they would have killed us by now.'

The women turned to Joe, puzzled, distracted by his voice. This gave Cloake his cue. With a furious roar, he leapt at the women. His great bulk skittled them to the floor and knocked Chepi's rifle flying. In a second, he had each of them by the hair and cracked their skulls together, the dull choc of bone on bone. Without a second's hesitation, the women buried Cloake under a storm of punches, raw, wild strength. He rolled on top of Chepi like a fallen ox, let go her hair and seized the rifle. Kimana made a grab for the barrel and tried to wrestle the gun free. In the confined space of the barn, the sound of the rifle going off was like dynamite in a mine. The horses reared and bucked, whinnied in terror.

Cloake tried to swing the rifle butt at Chepi's skull as he scrambled to his feet. Kimana clung to the barrel with one hand and flailed punches with the other. Every time Cloake jerked the gun free and elbowed himself away, she fought back. He kicked her aside, she threw herself at him. He swung the rifle at her face, she ducked and butted him in the gut, made him reel. Blood ran from a gash on her cheek where the rifle caught her, but she ignored it. Cloake was backed up against the wall. Again, Kimana made a grab for the rifle barrel with one hand, and flung punches with the other. Chepi forced herself up off the floor.

Joe saw what was going to happen. The women were fearless, they would never give up. But the way Cloake was swinging the rifle butt, one of them was going to get her skull stove in. Joe hacked at the remains of the rope. He yelled at Cloake to stop, to put down the gun, there was no need for this. Then suddenly, the last strands of rope gave way. On his feet, his leg wrapped in fire, he lurched at the three of them. He yelled at Cloake, seized Chepi, who was nearest him, by the shoulder and flung her out of the way. Then he grabbed a fistful of Kimana's buckskin shirt, ready to heave her aside so he could get to the rifle and wrench it out of Cloake's hands.

Still gripping the rifle barrel, Kimana wasn't going to give up now. Chepi threw herself at Joe. His leg buckled, burst with pain, and he catapulted backwards on the floor. Holding on to her shirt, Joe dragged Kimana backwards, down on top of him. Cloake saw his opportunity. He swung the rifle butt over his head and aimed to hammer it down on her where she lay spread-eagled on top of Joe. With one great heave Joe rolled them both to one side. Cloake's rifle butt slammed into the dirt. Chepi swung wildly at Joe and clipped his cheek with her fist, enough for his vision to blur. Kimana elbowed him in the gut, tore herself free and with an unearthly scream launched herself at Cloake one more time.

Joe pulled himself to his feet. He grabbed Kimana's shirt again and held on. Chepi leaped on his back, beat at his arm with her fist to make him let go. Then the blast from a handgun made everyone freeze. Chepi slid down off Joe's back, Cloake steadied his rifle, Kimana let go her hold on the barrel, Joe still clutched a fistful of Kimana's shirt. Rowan Gold stood in the doorway of the barn, and beside him was Grace.

Gold shoved his Colt hard into Joe's chest. He stared him in the eyes like an avenging angel.

'Let her go,' he roared.

Joe released the handful of buckskin shirt and

took a pace back. Gold didn't lower his gun. Free from Joe holding on to her, Kimana pulled back her right arm and let an uppercut fly. Her fist drove into Cloake's jaw like a hammer. There was a crack, the sound of splintering teeth. Cloake's knees buckled and he crashed to the ground like a felled tree.

'Gracie?' Joe's heart leaped. His sister looked different, buckskin shirt and pants, her hair tied back, a bowie knife shoved in her belt. But it wasn't just the clothes – there was a look in her eye, something about her expression. He noticed it right away, but couldn't say what it was.

'Joe?' Grace stared in disbelief. 'What are you doing here?'

'I came for you, Gracie.' It was all he could think of saying.

The deer-hide bandage on Joe's leg, seeing him stagger, Grace was open-mouthed. Gold holstered his gun and turned his attention to the two Shoshone women.

'What happened? Are you hurt?' Grace was wide-eyed. 'What did you do to your leg?' Questions tumbled out of her. She beamed at him, her delight to see him was obvious. She slipped her arm under his shoulder and helped him across to the hay pile. That smile. That was the smile Joe had held in his imagination, that was the smile that had appeared in his dreams. And now here was Gracie, with her arms round his shoulders, kissing him on the cheek. Inside his chest, his heart banged for joy.

A second woman had appeared in the doorway, leading two horses. She looped the reins expertly round the door handle and hurried in. Older than Grace, tall and strong, there were streaks of grey in her auburn hair. She also was dressed in buckskin clothes, the same as Grace and the Shoshone women. She had a determined set to her jaw and studied the scene carefully, worked out for herself what had gone on. She stepped over Cloake's bulk where he lay on the floor as if she hadn't noticed him, and hurried over to Grace.

'This is my brother Joe.' Grace smiled. 'He came up here to find me.'

'Friend of yours?' The woman nodded in the direction of where Cloake lay.

'Trailed me all the way up here,' Joe said. He thought about Cloake undoing the tourniquet and leaving him lying in the dust. 'Intended to take back Grace, till the Shoshone women got him.'

Grace had been so delighted to see Joe, she hadn't registered who the other man was till now. She looked over at him and caught her breath.

'Don't you worry, Gracie,' the woman assured her. 'He won't be taking you anywhere.'

'You know him?' Joe was surprised.

'Didn't you hear about him getting his fingers shot off?' The woman smiled wryly. 'That's Jehu Cloake, and I have the great misfortune to be his wife.'

Over by the door, Gold was speaking in the Shoshone language to the two women, his words fast and urgent. He kept glancing at Cloake and over at Joe. He was making up his mind about something while they described to him what had gone on.

'So, this is the brother we've all heard about?' Gold strode over to Joe. He leaned down to shake Joe by the hand. Gold was tall, square-shouldered, with an easy manner and a friendly smile. Whatever trouble there was, he could deal with it. The wary look in his eye meant he could see if someone wasn't talking straight. 'Ordinarily I don't allow visitors. Kimana and Chepi tied you up because they didn't know what to do with you.'

'They saved my life,' Joe indicated his leg. 'Would have bled out it they hadn't found me.'

Later, Gold sat with Joe. The cabin held the homely smell of coffee and woodsmoke. It was a simple place, log built, with a fire grate and one window protected by a wooden shutter. There were a couple of neatly folded blankets by the hearth, a bed covered in beaver pelts in the corner, a table and chairs. A hunting rifle stood by the door. The shutter was propped open, the range of pine-clad mountains rolled away into the distance, beyond them the snowy peaks sparkled in the morning sunlight.

'So, you came up here in search of your sister,' Gold said.

'Word in the saloon was that you were holding her prisoner,' Joe said. 'But I can see it ain't like that.'

Gold stared out of the window, at the pines, the mountains and the sky.

'Gracie looks well,' Joe wanted Gold to know how grateful he was. 'I'm obliged to you for looking out for her. I'll get her home, buy her some new clothes and everything will be fine.'

'Is that what they say about me? That I kidnapped her?' Gold stared at Joe, half puzzled, half amused. 'What about Sarah Cloake? They say I'm holding her prisoner, too?'

'I didn't know what to believe.' Joe floundered. 'Saloon talk was all the information I had.'

'What else do they say about me?'

'I . . .' Joe hesitated. If he didn't tell the truth, Gold would know. 'That you killed a man, that you're hiding out from the law up here.' Then he added, 'That you took two Shoshone wives.'

Gold turned back to the view of the mountains.

Joe didn't know whether he had said too much.

'Two wives? Is that what they're saying?' Gold didn't seem surprised. 'Only time I go into town is to trade at the store, pelts for supplies. I call in at the saloon while I'm there, but there's too many rules in town for my liking – laws, bibles, bar-room gossip, somebody always telling you how you ought to live. Things are simple in the mountains: you either survive or you don't. And if you do, this is your reward.' He nodded towards the window. The pale sky was streaked with cirrus cloud as fine as gauze, rose pink in the rising sun. High on the thermals, an eagle circled. The peaks glistened molten gold in the morning light.

'I saw the notice chalked on the saloon wall, didn't think much to it at the time. When I told Sarah, she was outraged, said she had a soft spot for Grace ever since she was a girl. She guessed what your pa was up to, and she was certain Jehu would be the first one to put in a bid. Told me to get back down there and put a stop to it.'

'Well, like I said, I'm obliged.' Joe meant it sincerely, but his words sounded weak.

From outside in the yard came the sound of the women's laughter. After some discussion they had decided to take a mug of coffee out to Cloake who was, once again, tied up in the barn.

'Question is,' Gold looked Joe straight in the

eye. 'Why didn't you stop your pa?'

'I didn't know.' Joe's answer was quick off his tongue. 'How could I? Gracie didn't even know herself. He'd planned this, weeks ahead. You saw the notice on the saloon wall.'

Joe felt uncomfortable, he was being accused when he had done nothing wrong.

'I was busy. There was the fishing. Had to tend to my traps every day. Pa did nothing except drown in his own red eye.' Joe realized his words sounded like an excuse. He changed the subject. 'You killed a man. That's why the law's after you, that's why you live up here.'

'I did kill a man,' Gold said calmly. 'It was a long time ago. We played a poker hand and I beat him fair and square. He said I was cheating, and called me out. Just like your pa, he drew on me first.'

'Pa got what was coming to him.' Joe had never actually said that before, out loud or to himself. It pained him to say it about his own kin, but it was true. He remembered his father's body lying on a trestle at the back of the saloon, coins on his eyes.

Gold got up and stared out of the window.

'Storm on its way,' he said.

Joe followed his gaze, but he couldn't see anything except blue sky and sunshine.

'Be here in a couple of hours,' Gold went on. 'Spring mornings, warm winds roll down off the mountains as strong as a tornado. Some days, they melt a foot of snow in an hour.'

'It won't settle in, will it?' Suddenly anxious, Joe stared out at the sky. 'I plan to take Gracie home as soon as I can.'

12

Within an hour, the storm hit. A gale kicked up
dust in the yard so that the sky was obscured by a
brown mist. The blast howled in the canyon, a dis-
sonant chime against the moans and cries from
the gullies higher up the slopes. The great
Ponderosas creaked and heaved under the strain;
their branches swayed and whipped, sometimes
unearthly notes sang between them, sometimes
they roared like surf on a rocky shore.

Gold took the Shoshone women out to the barn
to calm the horses. Inside the cabin, Sarah closed
the shutter tight and laid a rolled blanket at the
foot of the door to keep out the dust. She set to
work making bread for them all. Sleeves rolled up,
she covered the table in flour and began to work
the dough. The wind moaned in the chimney;

when she lit the cooking fire, the flames rattled in the flue.

'I asked him to take me.' Grace smiled at Joe's question, she could see the concern in his face.

'You ran out of the saloon and called out as he came by?' Joe sat on the floor by the grate, his leg stretched out. Grace knelt beside him.

'Didn't know where I was going right then. How could I?' Grace was patient with him. 'I was running, all I knew was I had to get away.' She took her brother's hand in hers to show him he was worrying when there was no need. 'Pa told me he'd fixed up for me to go and work on one of the other farms for the spring. He said I'd get paid something and it would leave only two mouths to feed at home. It made sense. Only thing was, he wouldn't tell me which farm. He said we were heading to the saloon to finalize arrangements.'

Joe looked grave. He studied his sister's face – her calm blue eyes seemed untroubled by the story of what had happened to her, a smile always played at her mouth.

'I knew Pa was up to something,' Grace continued. 'He said there was going to be a contract. I thought that meant he would try to wangle some kind of down payment.'

'And you went along with it?'

'Why not?' Grace shrugged. 'Thought I would

be making money for the family doing the same work I would be doing at home anyway. It was just for a season. I thought maybe this time one of Pa's schemes was going to pay off.'

'Then he put you up for auction.' The words were like stones in Joe's mouth.

Outside, the wind screamed. There was a layer of dirt on the cabin floor, as fine as sand. It came in through the walls, round the edges of the window shutter; nothing could stop it. Grace took her hand away from Joe's.

'I didn't know, Gracie,' Joe said. 'How could I?'

'You kept away from him.' Grace stared at him. 'You were always hiding out in the barn, out fishing, out with your traps. You left me to deal with him, sometimes you avoided him for days.'

Joe felt the accusation. He should have looked out for his sister. If he had stood up to his pa, taken charge, taken responsibility, worked with him to make the farm run at a profit, none of this would have happened. He saw it now, as clear as day.

'When I ran out of that saloon, I knew Pa had been shot, I didn't realize he was dead.' This troubled Grace. 'All I could think was, I had to get away from Jehu Cloake.'

'Amen to that.' Sarah laughed. She had loaded the dough into the Dutch oven to prove. Her hands were white with flour. 'Rowan found me walking on the trail the night I lit out. I hoped a wagon would come along and I could talk them into giving me a ride to California. Instead, he brought me back here. Kimana and Chepi looked after me.'

'Lucky man to have two wives,' Joe said.

'Wives?' Grace scoffed. 'Where did you hear that? That's typical saloon talk. Rowan lived with the Shoshone when he first came up here. He was out hunting with one of the braves when a bear attacked, had the brave in its claws. Rowan shot the bear and saved the brave's life. Kimana and Chepi are his sisters. They helped Rowan build the cabin and the barn, and now they're teaching him the Shoshone way of tracking, everything he needs to survive. They see it as paying back a debt on behalf of their family and the whole village. They're proud to do it.'

'I just want to get you home,' Joe said. 'Buy you some proper clothes, then we can go on like before.'

'Buckskin's fine.' Sarah overheard him. 'Warm, practical. I spent years sheep farming in a cotton dress and underskirts. You should try it.'

Joe laughed, a ridiculous notion.

'You don't have to worry about your sister being around Rowan Gold. He's a decent man,' Sarah said. 'Take it from me, I know what the other sort's

148

like. I had fifteen years with Jehu.'

Outside, the wind had dropped, the moan in the canyons faded and left only the creak and sway of the high branches. Sarah lifted the shutter and peered out. The sky was blue and clear; the peaks glowed like flame in the morning sun.

'Old Jehu was a tough one, I always knew that. In the early days, he was ambitious, we both were. Worked day and night to build that farm. Sheep up on the high plains in summer, down with us in the winter. I did the farm work, looked after the flock alongside him, and I kept house.'

Sarah emptied the dough out of the Dutch oven on to the table, and started to knock it back. When she had finished, she shaped it, loaded it back into the oven and stood the iron pot at the edge of the fire.

'Over the years, the farm did well. Jehu was a good manager, kept his flock alive through the winter, always came out on top when he made a deal. But his ambition turned to meanness.' Sarah chose her words carefully, it was something she had thought about for a long time. 'Wouldn't spend money on hiring a hand, cheaper to send me up to the high plains instead. We had arguments. Trivial things, big things; his dinner didn't taste right, whether we should buy more breeding ewes. Whatever the cause, he never wanted to part

149

with a single bill from the roll he kept in his vest pocket. The arguments turned to fights. I gave as good as I got.' Sarah looked across at Joe. 'He tell you I shot his fingers off, the night I left?'

Joe nodded. He remembered the men in the saloon laughing behind their hands, never to Jehu's face.

'Bet he never told you he was coming at me with a horsewhip when I snatched his gun.'

The door opened suddenly. Gold and the two Shoshone women crossed the room to warm themselves at the fire.

'Smells good in here, Sarah.' Gold held his open palms over the flames, then rubbed his hands together. 'Storm's dropped, so I'm going to send Jehu on his way.'

Sarah seemed not to hear him. She knelt down and prized open the lid of the Dutch oven to check on the loaf.

'He's in the barn saddling his horse right now. Told him to come across and pick up a canteen when he's done. Can't send a man off without water.'

Neither Grace nor Joe spoke. After Sarah's story, neither of them wanted to hear mention of Jehu Cloake's name. Sarah busied herself with the fire. A few minutes later, there was the sound of hoofbeats in the yard. When the door opened again,

Cloake stood there. The swelling over his eye had gone down; the skin was stained where a herb poultice had been held on it.

'You going to give me some of that?' Cloake nodded towards the Dutch oven.

'It ain't ready.' Sarah got to her feet.

'We won't send you away empty-handed.' Gold held out a canteen. He nodded to Kimana, who produced a pouch of herbs from her belt.

'Don't want your stinking herb remedies.' He knocked Kimana's hand aside.

Gold stepped in: 'Break him off a piece of bread, then he can go.'

Cloake's anger was palpable. His eyes blazed, the corners of his mouth turned down in a sneer. He glared at each of them in turn to make sure they all felt his contempt. Then his gaze settled on Gold.

'I didn't ride all the way up here for a hunk of burnt bread and a canteen of water. I came for what's mine.' His shoulders dropped slightly, like a boxer, aggressive and ready.

'I'm letting you go. I'm giving you supplies.' Gold's voice was matter-of-fact, as if he was checking off a list. 'Be grateful for it.'

'I want my money and I want my gun.' Cloake glared at him. 'And I want her.' He nodded at Grace. 'I made a deal with her pa.'

Suddenly, the only sound in the room was the spit of the fire.

'You never know when to quit, do you?' It was Sarah's voice. She stood beside Gold, her back to the fire. 'Even when you're treated better than you deserve, you always want more.'

'I worked day and night for that money.' Cloake ignored her and stared at Gold. 'Made a farm out of wilderness, singlehanded, no hired hands, not even at lambing time. It was always just me. You took that roll of bills out of my hand.' He nodded to Grace. 'Get out to the barn and saddle your horse.'

'I was never for sale, Jehu.' Grace's voice was like steel.

Joe tensed. He would like nothing better than to launch himself at Cloake, bad leg or no.

'All right then.' Cloake turned back to Gold. His mouth twisted in a smirk. 'What if I let you keep the girl to add to your collection? Give me my gun and my money, and I'll be on my way.'

'The money's Sarah's,' Gold said flatly. 'When you get home you'll have the farm, all she's got is a roll of bills.'

'My Colt. Let me have that.' Cloake wouldn't give up. 'There's wolves about. I might need it.'

Gold thought for a minute, then pulled back the pelt on the bed. Cloake's handgun was underneath.

'Rowan, what are you doing?' Sarah pulled at his arm. 'Don't give him a gun.'

Joe and Grace chimed in to try and dissuade him. Kimana and Chepi took a pace back; Kimana's hand was on the bowie in her belt.

Rowan flicked open the chamber and emptied the shells into his hand. He held the Colt and shells out to Cloake.

'You can reload when you're on your way.'

Cloake shoved the handgun in his belt and tipped the shells into his jacket pocket. His face looked as though it had been carved out of lead, grey, sagging cheeks, dark rings under his eyes. The canteen was looped over his shoulder.

'What about something to eat?' His voice was gravel.

Gold nodded to Sarah. For a second everyone turned towards her as she lifted the lid on the oven, and a cloud of the sweet, good smell of fresh-baked bread filled the room. In that moment, Cloake snatched the rifle that was propped by the door. In the time it took for them all to focus, the rifle was at Cloake's hip, the barrel directed straight at Grace.

Pandemonium. It seemed like everyone was yelling. Gold snatched his Colt out of its holster, Kimana's bowie was in her hand. In the confusion, Sarah stepped back, knocked over the iron pot and the burning hot lid clattered in the grate. Joe launched himself at Cloake, fists bunched. Cloake sidestepped, forward not back, grabbed Grace by the arm and yanked her into Joe's path. He cannoned into her; Grace yelled. Trying to turn, to avoid crashing his sister to the floor, Joe's flailing arm knocked Gold's gun hand. A wild shot from the Colt exploded into the floor. Cloake held Grace out in front of him now, at arm's length, a bunch of her hair clenched in his fist. He forced her head down to make her to drop to her knees while he brought the rifle up with his other hand and aimed the tip of the barrel where the skull meets the spine.

'No, no please. She ain't done nothing.' Joe's arms were outstretched. He knew what Cloake was capable of, knew he had never backed down in his life: he would rather shoot Grace than hand her over. 'I'll get you your money.'

Cloake glanced towards him, a flicker of interest. But his eyes were on Gold, whose Colt was still in his hand.

'Put down the rifle and we'll buy her.' Joe was desperate. 'Sarah will give you the money. Just hand her over.'

The sweet smell of the bread had turned to the bitter stink of burning. Something had caught beside the grate. The lid from the oven had rolled on to the blankets. There was black smoke in the air.

Grace struggled, flailing with her arms to get Cloake to let go. She cried out as he gave the fistful of her hair one more vicious twist and jabbed the rifle barrel harder against the back of her skull.

'Get the money.' Cloake couldn't resist. Something like a smile played on his lips. 'Tell him to put his gun away.'

'Do as he says.' Joe turned to Gold. 'Sarah, give him the money.'

Beside the grate, the blankets had caught. The stink was acrid, orange flames followed the line of the weave.

'Put that damn fire out.' Cloake took charge. The smoke caught in all their throats and stung their eyes. Grace coughed as if her lungs were fit to burst, she had to fight for each breath. When she tried to cry out her voice was cracked, hardly more than a whisper. 'Shut up.' Cloake shook her. The more she struggled, the tighter he choked her.

Kimana kicked the iron lid back on to the grate and turned the blankets over. A cloud of smoke and dust billowed up.

'Where's my money?' Cloake was out of patience. With his arm tight across her throat, Grace couldn't breathe.

'Here.' It was Sarah's voice. Gold stood aside to

let her through. In her left hand, she held out a
roll of bills.

For a second, Cloake loosened his grip on Grace
to take them. As Sarah pressed the greenbacks into
Cloake's hand, Joe grabbed Grace and pulled her
away. Cloake's fist tightened on the money. He
yelled half in triumph at getting the money, half in
anger at feeling Grace slip out of his grasp. Gold's
hand flew for his gun but his holster was empty: his
gun was in Sarah's right hand, levelled at Cloake.
She pulled the trigger.

As Cloake crashed to the floor, a red stain
flooded the front of his shirt. There was a look of
surprise on his face. Even with a gun pointed
straight at him, the notion that anyone, let alone
his wife, might get the better of him was incon-
ceivable to him. Grace snatched the rifle out of his
hand and covered him, ready to blast him if he
moved. But Cloake lay still, the roll of bills
clutched in his fist.

The sun was high when Joe waited outside the
cabin. Goodbyes were always difficult. Gold and
the others stood there with him while Grace
fetched Magic from the barn. The pair of saddlebags slung over Joe's shoulder were packed with
trail food, pemmican, dry buffalo meat and bread;
Sarah made sure he had everything he needed.

Gold had presented him with Cloake's Colt and ammunition; the gun was shoved in his belt. Kimana had inspected his wound again and rebandaged his leg. They had all asked him to stay.

'Do you want me to take . . . back to town?' Joe said. Talking about Cloake's body with Sarah standing there embarrassed him.

'No need. I'll find a place for him further up the canyon. Rowan will give me a hand.' Sarah paused and stared at the ground, her shoulders slumped as if a great yoke was pressing on them. 'All in all, I got no regrets. The past is the past, that's what they say, ain't it? I won't think of Jehu often, but when I do, I'll try to remember the early days before everything went sour. Tell you one thing though, he rode up the canyon with hatred in his heart and got payback for everything he's done.' After a moment, she looked up and forced herself to change the subject. 'Where's that girl got to?'

Everyone looked in the direction of the barn.

'So much to do on the farm.' The silence was awkward, Joe did his best to fill it. 'You sure you don't want to change your mind?'

'I'm never going back,' Sarah said firmly. 'I want you to take on Jehu's flock – that will be a good start for you right there. I'm happy to provide it.'

They all watched the Shoshone women stretch the blanket out flat and cut round the burn, ready to make a repair.

Grace led Magic out of the barn, saddled up and ready. For once, her smile was missing, her face was solemn.

'I ain't coming, Joe.' Grace handed him the reins. 'I thought you'd be staying on a day or two to give me the chance to explain.

'What are you talking about?' Joe felt weak, the words were a knife in his heart. But somewhere, deep down, this was what he expected to hear.

'Grace made her plans before you got here,' Gold said gently.

Joe searched the faces of the others. Sarah, Kimana, Chepi, they all knew.

'Me and Sarah plan to join up with a wagon train and head to California,' Grace lifted the saddlebags off Joe's shoulders and tied them behind Magic's saddle.

'We're going to find somewhere and open a saloon.' She beamed with pride at the idea. 'You can come visit. Everyone's welcome.'

Looking at his sister standing there in her buckskin suit, her hair in braids, Joe knew he had been right the minute he first saw her up here. She had changed, and there was no changing back.

'The farm,' Joe stumbled over his words. 'Half of it's yours. It's your home, ain't it?'

'I'm done with the farm, Joe.' Grace's voice was

gentle, but there was self-assurance in her words, the strength of having come to a decision. 'Since Ma died, I've worked, kept house, cooked and cleaned for you and Pa every day. I ain't doing that no more.'

'Gracie. . . .' Joe knew there was nothing he could say.

'Sarah's got enough money to get us started.' Excitement made her talk faster, words spilled out of her. 'We're going to call the place The Lucky Star Saloon. We'll have everything, good whiskey, proper food. There'll be a kitchen out back which serves up dinners with thick gravy, the way people like. There'll be a piano so we can have music if anyone comes along who can play. There'll be tables for cards. . . .'

'We'll keep a shotgun under the bar,' Sarah interrupted fiercely. 'We won't put up with any nonsense.'

'Gonna be the best behaved saloon in the country, I can vouch for that,' Gold said. They all laughed.

'When will I see you, Gracie?' A stone weighed in Joe's heart.

'I know you'll miss me. I'll miss you too, Joe.' She reached up and kissed him lightly on the cheek. 'But this is my chance for the life I want to live. You've decided to make a success of the farm, and Sarah's helped you do it.'

As Joe reached the entrance to the yard, he turned in the saddle and looked back. There they all were, staring after him. Grace had made her plans, there was hope in her heart, and she was safe and happy. Wasn't that all he wanted for her? Wasn't that why he had ridden up here?

Joe couldn't bring himself to wave goodbye.